Table of Contents

Namaste

Namaste

Dedications:

God Bless all y'all youngsters out there, slaving away learning your instruments; your music lessons. I gotta lotta love and admiration for you all. Only some of you will get bitten by "The Bug" and aspire to become a professional, serious musician or performer.

"Working," practicing your instruments or your vocals is like those people who get addicted to jogging; they get past a certain point and a euphoric sensation surges through them. Same thing in practice – you get good enough where you can start creating your own riffs and then you really begin enjoying the "work." You can play for hours; long past exhaustion into that euphoric zone that the long distance runner hits.

If you have talent; if you have been given "a gift," and you **do the work**, someday you can contribute

Namaste

to the vast and extraordinary catalogue of America's greatest contribution to the planet; to the Solar System; to the species: Popular music.

Thanks Anne Hathaway on Fiverr.com for the Photoshop work. Contact her: https://www.fiverr.com/annetouch

Playlist Elizabeth: on Spotify

https://play.spotify.com/user/12159501044/playlist/1hISAJWIzdhrTv2oM78OXa

Namaste

Prologue

Hmm hmm (singing softly) *hmm hmm…*

Time has let go of you, nothing will ever change;

no difference between today, tomorrow or yesterday.

Hmm hmm… hmm hmm… Time has let go of you …

"We worked on that, remember?"

"God… I'm too young to be putting flowers on my lovers' grave; your grave. I'm too fucking young for this! Oh God, oh. Oh God this fucking sucks. I don't know how I'm gonna… I'ma try baby, I guess I'll just, you know, try to do this."

"I'm not coming back here to see you anymore; you know, too agonizing."

Namaste

"It really does hurt, like a fucking arrow through the heart. "

I have the place my heart use to be; the ribs are broken, the skin got torn when my heart shot out of my chest. The space is filling up with xanny bars and rum. Nothing but white noise raging in my thoughts. "Dasa anu dasa," I can't interrupt my thought stream with all those tricks you taught me. You know, I need a baseline close to peace; I'm nowhere near that now. I need to negotiate an armistice with my consciousness; hence, the xanny, the rum.

I can't sleep. I can't wake up. I have to resuscitate my flat lined soul into what I pass off as alive, these days. I have to summon something from deep in my psychic core to resist swallowing a handful of oblivion; shhh, and let it pass. Though there are more days surrendering to the spring sun, today the sky is slate; in contrast to the bright white marble that marks your eternal address.

Namaste

Ima thinking that this thing is gonna be with me my whole entire life. Everybody tells me how yes, it hurts so much right now, but that time will heal this gaping wound. There will come a time when I can watch a rom com and laugh; I will notice that there are other men out there; that they are looking over at me and I will flash them that smile I used only for you. I will slowly emerge from this fog of despair when the warmth of the day star, rays of love burn off the cold wet sadness which bogs me down. My friends tell me how I will, perhaps in a month, or a year, find myself suppressing the utter soul numbing grief, allowing my heart to spring up with the warmth of those rays. As it is, now, I can only taste the sour fruits produce of the seeds of despair watered and fertilized with my aching tears. My love lover fiancé, my man, first man, only man, my m8 paramour my world my protector, raison d'être…

Namaste

I don't know where to begin; the end hasn't ended and is still confusing; so I guess, you know, at the beginning; genesis: What a year. I went from being as insignificant as a bug is to the universe, to well, a larger bug, more complex, with thoughts and dreams. The oldest illusion in the book; I could see a light up ahead; about to emerge from the dark tunnel. It turns out to be an oncoming train.

"I am going to London babe, and complete the deal," (blowing my nose.) "I know all I got right now is your- our material you and I... well, we did the big work. So much of this is you; when I finish, you will live on."

"I'ma crash at your pad in Queens for a bit; get away from all the drama and stress, and my wailing mother."

"I'm sorry. She's sorry. I don't believe she would've said anything if she thought things

Namaste

would get like this baby. She's worse off than me… I've gotta worry about her now. I said some tough things. Blamed her…"

"She hovered over me for a couple of days because I was sick; uh, vomiting, and dizzy and all that. Well, I told her it was the grief, I thought it was, but she made me pee on the stick. It showed '+'."

"Oh man, I didn't think of… You should've seen her. Went totally white and her eyes bugged out."

"I freaked out, screamed at her 'What are you gonna do, have him arrested! That would be better! I wish you would have! Before fuckin dad!'"

She left and I haven't talked to her since.

"Well, I've told you what I had to tell you; I gotta jet babe."

Chapter 1

That's not My Name:

One of those minor yet persistent questions which follow a person through their life is how different would I be if I had a different name. Although my name is Elizabeth, my p's call me *liz-a-beth*. I always thought that if you're gonna say 3 syllables of my name, how much more effort is it to include the *E*; which is what my friends call me; or occasionally they'll call me E squared for the 2 E's in my name, Elizabeth Erickson. When I was 12, I asked my p's if I could legally change my name from Elisabeth, which is what I was given at birth and on my birth certificate   e, to Elizabeth. At that time they owed me; so we did it. We filled out the forms; paid the fee; published it in the paper; went to the hearing. Cost $65.00 to change an 's' to a 'z.'

Some teachers call me Beth or Liz, or they'll say "*A ha, like the Queen of England!*" Dependent upon my mood, I'll shoot back "*which one!*" I prefer the reference to the 1st one, the virgin queen; not the now one.

Due to the fact that I live way out here, in the boonies, all I have is like one close friend. All I basically do is eat, sleep, practice; and study and work on the farm; isn't that so thrilling; come join my world.

"Lizabeth, could you do me a favor and get a 1% milk and a can of cat food on your way home from your lesson sweetheart," my mom yells out from somewhere inside the house.

I've had my cat Tiger since I was a baby and she only eats that smelly Friskies canned cat food. My mom asked again when I come inside the house. She kisses me on my head and hands me the blue Visa card to pay for the class. 11:30 every

Saturday, I drive myself to my guitar lesson at The Music Depot in the mall.

I've been taking lessons for almost 2 years; since I was like 12. "Sure mom," I answered, "could I use the card to get some stuff while I'm there?"

"What are you gonna get" she asked.

I told her nothing specific, "just some snacks with my friends."

"Don't spend too much, I think there's maybe $100 or so on the card" she then explained, "and after you pay for your lesson, you have to put gas in your truck."

"Okay mom, I'll be back before 2, love ya!" Many times I would meet up with some friends at the mall after my lesson; but today I'm gonna crash early because I have like a terrible headache ominously descending upon me already. Like some vortex obeying the laws of angular momentum, things are getting closer and closer, tighter and tighter, and spinning faster and faster until its resolution crashes into everything that comes close.

I downed 3 Advils; I'd usually take more but I'm all out; I have to remember to buy some more Advil Gel Caps or face the daunting prospects of allocating the rest of my day dealing with the elephant sitting on my dome.

I live with my p's Lillian and Daniel; no brothers, no sisters. I am living the nightmare of my mother's dream; residing on her farm, with like a thousand animals.

It's my mom's fantasy lifestyle. As a consolation, I know that life for me could be even worse; my mom really would like to live off grid in Alaska, as deep into the bush as possible. She always talks about the excitement and the challenge of living in total wilderness; subsiding off the produce of the nature world, and one's own cleverness and stamina; she's a prepper; you know, like for doomsday.

The universe has spared me that ultimate cruelty of desolation living but teases me by staging my birth in this place which is close enough to my dream where I can see the bubble of light pollution hovering to the east on a foggy or low cloud night. Each transcontinental flight begins its descent overhead, reminding me that I live close enough to dream it; but flights going west are mid-ascent which goad me that I still live in the fringe of fly over country.

I should thank mom for throttling her dream, somewhat. Yeah, right; if she were to convince my dad to fully live that life, I would've split from that scene as soon as I could drive; that's not my dream; actually, it's the opposite of my dream; a dreadful night terror.

My friend Pepper and I talk, and have basic plans re: wanting to live in the city. We want urban modernity, check; we want the sass, check; we want the sizzle, check; we'd like to become citiots, double check. After this school year, I'm going to get my GED so I can leave school early, check again. Deep down in my soul, I get that foreboding sense that bottom line, Pepper will be a casualty, lost along the way; I don't feel the drive in her.

My dad used to live and work in the city. He use to work as some kind of technical person for different businesses; I think with communications and computers. After a while, my mom convinced him to come and live with us out in the sticks and help run this place. So now he sort of works part of the time there, and most of the time he's here. Even when he's here though, he's like an animal who's off licking his wounds; the city, and his life has chewed him up.

He does his best to try and discourage me from my plan to eventually base myself in the city. He explains how I will disappear into the supermassive vortex; because I am female, I will wind up property of some sadistic pimp in the porn industry.

Well fuck daddy, I fit the stereotype I'd yell at him. He hasn't sexually raped me, but he has tried. Stupid dick, he gets all drunk or stoned or smacked up and he comes on to me. I easily can kick his douchebag drunk ass; and I think that's his real goal.

I don't know how much my mom is aware of his advances or his drug use. Is she blind; is she faking ignorance; is she being defensive? Anyway, I only use dope occasionally; bump a line to help with my stress and headaches.

I started out with stealing some of his smack stash; but I soon discovered how it's easier to take some buds and trade for dope or xanny or hydros. I am not a fan of bud, so this works out. He is really good at growing bud; and he has so much, like 50 plants: I can look over the little placards by each plant: Maui Waui, Amnesia Haze, GSK (ha, girl scout kooki), Lemon Haze; on and on.

Then there are his guns. He must have like 10 guns; pistols, rifles, and I think an AK. He let me shoot that and the pistol a lot when I was a kid. I definitely am gonna get a Beretta 9mm like he has; it's a beautiful gun, and as my dad says, it fits my hand perfectly.

I know it looks so noble from the outside that he didn't remain a deadbeat because he moved in, lives with and supports us; I'd prefer to be destitute and fatherless. I fear he's already wounded my soul and I am embarrassed that I am among the scores of cliché teen girls inappropriately touched by daddy.

My mom and dad aren't legally married, yet. When I was a kid, I questioned that whole relationship; and if my dad was my dad, and all that. After a long, multi-layered, convoluted story, I understood what was going on; I was so hoping he really wasn't my bio dad.

I've been there, to the city. I've seen a concert with my friends at the Garden. And then, when I was like 8, we all went to Radio City to see the Christmas show. It fucking rocked my world.

I don't have a driver's license yet, but my p's let me drive myself to the mall for my class; they let me drive around town, as long as it's daytime. I have been driving around the farm and my neighborhood since I was 12; one of the perks of living in such a rural area. Also, my p's are easy enough to manipulate, and get the results I want.

I pull into the gas station and pump gas into the truck. Now my hand smells like gasoline for my lesson, I should have waited till after class.

I grab my guitar out of the back seat and go into the mall towards the music store. My guitar is my dad's 1983 reissue of a 1957 California manufactured blackie Stratocaster with a custom tremolo and trem arm.

I like lugging my strat through the mall and have the kids from school checking me out. My guitar with the case must weigh around 30lbs; my teacher says I could use my acoustic guitar for my class because it is way lighter and all; but this guitar looks way cooler, and is easier to play.

Chapter 2

Life's Lessons:

"Hi ya doin' today Elizabeth?" Jeff, my guitar teacher asks.

"Hi Jeff, I smell like gas, sorry."

"Oh, I got you that new book; it has many more chords and some really cool scales, I think you are ready for it" he said holding up the big black book.

I smiled and said "thanks, but can I pay you for it next week, I didn't bring enough?" I was getting a new guitar book and it made me happy, it felt like progress, which meant distance from this place.

"No problem Elizabeth. You should also get another staff book for your theory classes at school, okay?"

I totally filled up my last book, not only with my homework but with a lot of tabs which I copped so I could learn some songs.

I've learned a lot of songs from watching people play them on YouTube. My dad has a lot of Fake books and sheet music of songs from the 1990's from his rock band days. Those books tell you what chords to play, but don't show the position of the chords, or the fingering, or how to transition between chords. I can always ask Jeff to show me stuff like *Under the Bridge* which we are working on today.

"So Elizabeth, how are your mother and father?"

"Um, they're just fine. My dad was playing the strat and said the strings are getting a bit gunky and I should put on a set of 8's."

"8's! those are really thin. You won't get any sound from them." Jeff protested.

"I know, I told him that. He said it would be easier to play."

"You're not playing only guitar solos on this," Jeff began to explain before I interrupted him.

"I know Jeff. He thinks they'd be easier for my little baby girl hands to play."

"What," Jeff asked and then continued "your dad doesn't know you have nice long strong fingers and you're developing some nice callouses there?"

"I told you Jeff, I'm pretty much on my own with this. My mom is happy about it but my dad hardly shows interest; except every once in a while, he'll play the strat. I can't wait to buy my own."

I believe that my father uses the excuse of wanting to play his guitar just to come in my room and have some 'father-daughter' time.

"At any rate, I don't have the money right now but I'll order the strings online next week."

I do have some bud I could sell; but I'm not like a dealer. I only sell it to people I know; people who ask me first.

Jeff is like a really cool dude, he takes me seriously and gives me good stuff to practice; he totally understands me and my dreams and aspirations. I like how he teaches me not only music theory, but all parts of music; guitar rhythm, leads and solos, improvisation, and scoring. We've even worked on some cool stuff like *Eruption*, the Eddie Van Halen solo, and *Enter Sandman*.

It is a good thing when you have a teacher who doesn't care that I am a girl. He doesn't dumb down my stuff because of being a girl.

My friends aren't into music like I am. I know lots of stuff from the 90's; mostly guitar orientated; my friends don't even know most of those songs. I grew up listening to that music.

My favorite time is at the end of the class when Jeff and I jam for like 10 or 15 minutes, and sometimes an hour. Jeff is always telling me how I have to develop thicker callouses on my fingers and how the muscles in my hands will remember what to do; and that is how you play smooth, with feeling, not having to think.

Food Court Convenes:

I wait at the food court with my guitar for Pepper after my class ends; my fingers still buzzing from that jam session. Believe me, jamming like that is quite a workout; I get all sweaty and my heart is racing; pumping unmedicated blood into my head; but it magnifies my head pain, big time.

I better call Pepper and see what's up.

"Hey E," she said after only one ring.

"Hey Pepper, ya comin?"

"Are you done with your guitar class now?" I told her I was and am waiting here. She said "5 minutes."

"Bye."

"Pepper, do you have any Advil," my skull is being crushed from the inside throbbing down my cervical spine.

"I got some xanny bars but no Advil sweetie," she pulls out her bottle from her bag.

"That's a new top? Very trippy, very colorful," I ask Pepper.

"Yeah, it's like all virgin-skankish, really bipolar" she giggled as she struck a pose with her butt sticking out.

"Well you got those super porno shorty shorts girly," Pepper said. "they're practically ripped all the way up; with your booty half hanging out!"

"Ooo, you got a thing for your teacher's thing!" Pepper said as she laughed.

"Nooo…, not quite Doctor Pepper."

Pepper's first name is Pepper, but her middle name is Birdsong. Her p's are full blown hippies and everyone in that family has a weird name. We call her sister Cindy Windy because her name is Cinnamon Windsong. They all have spicy first names and some sort of song middle names; yep, her p's are genuine tree huggers.

"You wanna get some big cookies" I said.

"Let's go" she said.

"I'm getting a mint chocolate chip ice cream cookie," I told her and then I changed my mind, "na, I'll get the iced cinnamon-oatmeal raisin cookie."

"Yummy!" Pepper said as she grabbed my hand pulling me to the cookie kiosk.

"Wait, my guitar" I barked out as I got it and followed her over.

"You know that boy Peter," Pepper asked.

"Long, streaky-blonde hair always wears that black hoodie" I stated.

Pepper explained "I thought he was sort of like a weird geeky emo kid, but I saw him talking and laughing with Carlos when I walked in before."

"Yeah Carlos knows him; Wait……What," I said a bit surprised. "Carlos is here?" I continued while pulling out my phone and dialing my bf's number.

"Oo, Pepper, how about you, you dirty girl, you just wanna tear into that zesty bod don't you," I chuckled.

"E-liz-a-beth! you're a major slut" Pepper said.

"You're trippin P," I snapped back while listening to the 3rd or 4th ring.

"Hey E, wassup?" Carlos said

"Carlos, you here at the mall?"

"That's right," he said and then he realized, "you have your lesson today, oh so then you're here E. Where you at" he then asked.

"Pepper and I are eating some cookies at the court."

"I'll come right over, okay." Carlos said, and made a kissing sound, then click.

"Peter is a senior like Carlos, and he's like single" I tell Pepper as he and Carlos come over to us.

"You two would make an alliterative couple – Peter and Pepper or Pepper n' Pete, you two should go out," I giggled.

"Just because you can get a hot senior bf E, we all can't be as hot as you."

"Want me to ask Carlos if he could set it up," I ask Pepper.

"You're talking like a lunachick E. He's a total fantasy, a senior, I'm a dorky freshman who…um hi guys," Pepper interrupted herself as the boys showed up.

"You play guitar Elizabeth," Peter blasts a smile as he asks me, pointing at my case.

I answer him briefly and try to direct his attention back to Pepper

"Pepper is a serious gamer at W-O-W Peter; she has her own subscription too; you two wanna go at it; see who is the deal?"

"Call of Duty you tard!" Pepper corrected me.

"World of Duty; Call of Warcraft; same difference. As you can tell, I'm not a gamer Peter," I joked.

That worked because the two of them are engaged in a conversation about gamer stuff. I hope he isn't like a total douchebag and insults her by saying something like she only plays the game because she only likes the changing the clothes part. I am totally not a gamer, no time, or interest.

I let those two chat, while I sidebar with Carlos about the possibility of a double date to set up Peter with Pepper.

After about 10 minutes of gamer speak, Carlos brings up the date.

"Awesome, I'm in. Oo, maybe we can go to that trampoline place that just opened," Carlos said.

"I never been, seems like fun," I say agreeing with the group. It would be enjoyable to go out with everyone, finally, for once.

"You mean *Bounce* or *Spring*; what's it called E?" Carlos asks.

"*Bounce*; they have that cool blacklights room with the music and stuff?" Peter answers.

Even though Pepper and I are close, major friends, we don't hang together very much like we used to. She has other friends that I don't know, or like that much, because they're not in my world, at all.

Actually, it's because I spend a lot of time on my music; it's not easy finding kids, or more specifically, girls my age who are interested in music professionally.

Besides, those girls are constantly having bitch sessions, kvetching about everyone, all the time. It's just so freaking boring to me. I'm committed to my music, it's a fast track outta this place, I hope.

Some days, I can practice 8 hours; I'd be playing and before I know it, 10 hours goes by. There have been nights when I start practicing after I get home from school, and then before I know it, I see the sky getting lighter and hear the roosters.

Pepper and Peter eventually share numbers and say goodbye. My head case is flaring up again.

"Dr. Pepper, I'll take that xanny bar for later if the Advil don't help cause I feel like I got a tumor in my head" I express with my pain voice.

She hands me the pill from her prescription bottle. "Thanks, I gotta jet Pepper," I say.

"Okay, later E. hope your head gets better," Pepper says as Carlos grabs my guitar.

"I got her!" I growl. I sounded ungracious of his gallant gesture, but I am very possessive of my guitar; don't want anybody else handling her. She is a female only because that's what it has been since it was my dad's guitar.

When I buy my own, it will certainly be a dude. I put the guitar in the truck and give Carlos a peck explaining "Oh man, I've gotta get home and down some drugs; my head is crushing me so bad I can't see straight."

Carlos gives me a sweet sympathetic peck on my cheek and says "Oh baby girl, I wish I could do something."

I tell him "You know I just got to get some meds in me and chillax and I'll be fine. I'll text you later when this freakin storm passes." After a couple more pecks on the cheeks and lips, I climb into my truck.

"I'm sorry babe, bye," I say, apologizing. He is such a prince to me considering that between my music the farm and his school sports obligations, we don't actually spend lots of time with each other; And then you throw in my head problems, I don't know why he digs me.

We have only gone out on a couple of dates and have only been going together for like maybe a month. Most of our relationship has been via texting and Skype.

I guess soon, one day when Carlos realizes how much time I put into music, and all the other stuff, he'll split the scene; of course after he tries to have sex. I know I'll probably spend my life alone, with my guitars; maybe giving guitar lessons – like Jeff. Maybe I could meet a cool guy like Jeff, someday; but he is married, and is like 40.

We played *Under the Bridge* for a half hour of the lesson; I keep thinking of those tragic lyrics. *Sometimes I feel Like I don't have a partner, Sometimes I feel Like my only friend, Is the city I live in, The city of angels, Lonely as I am, Together we cry.*

I like reading bio's of music celebs and see how they were discovered, how they broke through, how they ultimately made it. I have decided that I am definitely gonna have to leave here and take my talents to – well anywhere but here. No way I'm gonna be unearthed in this place.

Now my head hurts, DEFCON 1, let me take my meds.

Namaste

27

Chapter 3

The Storm Passes :

My mom hasn't been updated with the 'boyfriend' 411 yet because I'm really not sure about him. I should tell her, so she will get off my case about the 'boy situation.' She's always giving me the spiel about how now that I have grown boobs and am a woman, blah blah… and how the guys are gonna be blah blah blah blah…., as if I need it.

She was at the very least screwing at my age. She played Russian roulette and finally caught a live bullet at 15, got knocked up and here I exist. Mothers who get preggers young always overreact in their own daughter's protection schemes; they act as if their pregnancy was such a tragic shameful accident; to be avoided by the offspring at all costs; even as they speak face to face with that tragic shameful accident, me.

By the time I get home, the Xanvil combo is starting to kick in because I feel a lessening of the storm in my head. Looks like my mom is showing some stranger guy around; probably selling some chickens. Yikes, hope he doesn't rape my mom.

She has strangers come here often to buy or sell stuff with the animals. She's way too trusting sometimes. She has a Craig's List ad that brings some downright creepy dirt bags around here, doing farm business with my mom. This guy looks kinda hot; and I think he's taking a picture of me.

Woody's drive:

I have made an appointment to meet a girl about some chickens in New Jersey. She had a CL ad; I called, and so here I am driving from Queens to Sommerville New Jersey on a Saturday morning into afternoon.

So far there's been nothing but traffic problems from Queens into the city. Everything that could possibly get in my way has. I got every red lite, every slow poke and Asian driver; every rubber necker and looky-loo; every big rig with peeling recaps flying off; pot hole, buckled steel plates, cops, dui's, texters, and munching motorists; all conspiring to make me like 2 hours late.

My radio station has long since fizzled out so I scan for something not irritating. Times like this I wish I kept up my SiriusXM subscription, too late.

I'll take the tunnel, pop up on 42nd St., west side to the other tunnel, pop up in Jersey. That's like only halfway there; these hens better be spectacular. You can't order them online and ship them FedEx; well you can, if you order a bunch of little chicks; and then they aren't sexed; you could wind up with a henhouse of roosters.

I think I'll take the bridges on the way home; go open air for the girls; and hopefully, the one boy. A hundred miles from Manhattan is not just a different state, it's a whole new planet.

I'm wearing a new vintage DSOTM black tee, jeans, hi-top blue Chuck Taylors; I look like a farmer, I reckon. I gotta piss, fierce!

DESTINATION ON RIGHT, 1 MILE

"Thank God" I mumbled to the GPS.

I'm gonna pull over here to take a leak, there's no one and nothing around. Alright, I'm feeling better.

DESTINATION ON RIGHT

"Where… the hell…"

I turn into the drive; I can smell it, smells like, a farm. I check the phone to make sure I got bars; hmm, a hotspot too! I can see some of the birds.

Some look like white French poodles; and, I hear several cocks crowing!

Pictures of Lilli:

I see a woman who is strolling towards my truck; that must be her; not bad looking; she is actually pretty hot.

"Hello, you must be Woody, I'm Lilli" the blonde, green-eyed woman said holding out her hand.

"Yes; Hi Lilli" I said while grasping her hand; I'm thinking how my cat is named Lily and has green eyes.

"So you want a dozen silkie hens?"

I explained "I want silkies, but I'm also looking for some barred rocks or leghorns or reds if you have."

"Oh, and I'm in the market for a new rooster," I wanted to look around cause it looked like she had a lot of varieties.

"No problem, we can look around."

We stroll and chat as she points to the hen houses; it is bordered by a fence; it looks like she has the roosters tethered to a pole next to a small box, cock house? "I see" I said; "that's to keep them from fertilizing the hens?"

"Yep. And killing each other." she said.

So, I'm counting about a dozen box/poles, so 12 roosters. "12 roosters" I ask.

"I got more over there. Some are still too young to cause any damage so they run free," she explained.

As we walk around the farm I take some pics for future reference; especially the ones I took of Lilli. There are a lot of cool looking birds here. If I buy some of the big fatties, such as a barred rock, I won't have enough room in my portable cage for too many birds.

I tell Lilli more specifics of what I am looking for. I am really digging those big green eyes of hers;

with the golden hair and nicely tanned, and some very cute, strategically placed freckles on her cheek bones; she looks like a surfer girl; and she seems sweet.

Of course by this time I'm wondering if she is attached or not; I don't see a ring. That doesn't mean she doesn't have a boyfriend, or a baby daddy.

Ingénue:

I've been here about an hour, Lilli showing me the birds and the other animals around the farm and I'm taking pics of various birds so I can pick out which ones to buy. Click, click, click... I am taking pictures of some goats when abruptly, a circa 1980's F150 storms into the driveway.

Out of the cloud of dust and mass of scurrying insects dashes this golden-haired, guitar case carrying girl. In a smooth, discreet motion I pan my phone around to snap a couple of pics of her as she walked into the house.

I am familiar with that rectangular guitar case; it could be a strat, or a tele; either way, a girl playing an electric guitar is uncommon. They are heavy instruments considering the case and usually an amp also. Girls generally play acoustics because they are lighter to lug around.

That answers one question; Lilli's a baby momma; that was evidently her daughter. I was guesstimating that Lilli was approximately my age, but she has to be a bit older; so she had her daughter when she was very young. They share the same long golden hair and green eyes, only – holy shit, like the daughter's hair is practically to her knees.

I did not know that a human could grow that much hair, ever, never mind in perhaps 16 or 17 years.

My brain is going through a complex data processing equation right now, a Person Evaluation Algorithm (PEA), which will deliver an assessment to my consciousness based on the data my senses had maybe 5 seconds to take in.

She's nice and tall for a teen girl; 5 foot 10; maybe 11; some decent muscle tone and curves. She's like a buck twenty, nice top, black wife beater with jean short shorts, frayed around the legs;

Apple bottom jeans,

legs with the fray,

the whole place was looking her way, my mind's iPod plays while simultaneously processing the algorithm.

Chapter 4

Raccoon Bandits:

I had some pretty silkies years ago. Way before Martha Steward made them famous; she has made them in demand; and now the prices reflect that.

My birds always get killed by raccoons; I wanna fucking kill. Everyone else on the planet thinks raccoons are so cute with that face and the hands. Believe me they are fucking chicken killers.

They always seem to find clever ways, at night, to manipulate their way into the coop, which I close up every night when the birds mosey into their roost at sunset. Sometimes some of the birds decide to fly up a tree and want to stay out that night, but usually they all roost in the coop.

I've made a nice nesting situation in there; and I believe it's secure; but raccoons use those cute, dexterous hands to break into the coop and murder my girls. It's an arms race. They break in, slaughter, mayhem, and horror. They'll disembowel several birds; some birds fight back and survive; but are a witness to the awfulness committed on their sisters. I then see how the bastards broke in, reinforce my defenses, and on and on it goes.

So, the last bit of ultra-violence has led to me being here; they have all been massacred. I remember going outside in the dead of night with a super mega LED torch; I saw about 10 raccoons scramming up a tree and their eyes glowing back at me.

If I could have had and used a shotgun; blam blam you fuckers – I was practically foaming at the mouth with anger. I'm now prepared to use my bow and arrows; Ima nock a broadhead right into their guts.

Namaste

It was a complete horrorshow; all dead; even my glorious rooster – who had survived many raccoon invasions for over 10 years. He was a dear friend.

One time when he was younger he molted in mid-winter; walking around in the snow naked; even his comb dried up and fell off. I thought he was sick and would die; he grew new, more spectacular feathers, and a bigger redder comb; he was a glorious looking cock. His crow was so cute, he had his own voice; I knew it; I loved it.

Now I've redoubled my coop security and I am here, at this chicken farm in New Jersey, buying birds to replace the raccoon fodder.

Cranberry Sauce:

Lilli and I spent another half hour touring the farm. I've picked out 6 silkie hens and shoved them into the little cage in the back of my truck.

The farmer's daughter is sitting outside, under a big maple tree, singing along with something she's got playing in her buds.

You got me wrapped around your finger,

do you have to let it linger,

do you have to,

do you have to.

I recognize that old Cranberries' song.

"Nice singing," I blurt out to the girl; I do not know if she even heard me.

"Lizabeth, could you put out the pellets sweetheart" her mom asked the girl.

I assume the pellets are the feed for the chickens. I now know the name of the guitar toting girl. Unless, she has cat toys in the guitar case; naw, I don't think so.

Ten minutes go by and she was still singing along with what was playing in her buds. Some schoolgirl banging her head to … I can't recall the song she's singing now, but I know it's like 90's grunge.

Poor deprived thing – parents tortured her as a child whilst Fiona Apple or Sarah Mclachlan played as background music; she made a subliminal connection, and now she's developed some deviant behavioral characteristic association with any age and gender appropriate music.

I've never had a chick guitarist as a band m8 before. I've had chick m8s; usually they were vocals, occasionally some would play keyboards.

I'd like to talk to her, intro myself and explain that I'm a musician; I am always looking for other talented musicians; I am looking for someone to collaborate with; find out how serious she is.

I have to find out if she has talent as a singer or songwriter. I want to describe to her how I've been considering; shit, dreaming of a front man girl; although I hadn't imagined a front man virgin nymphet.

Shit, am I gonna need some twitterspeek dictionary or instagrammar to communicate in her slanguage.

DILEMA:

I gotta get rid of the mom; not 'rid of' I mean I need an opening line; I need some space. Realistically, I'd definitely be wary of me myself. She's like 17, and I'm some chicken buyer who is over 10 years older.

I'm sorta grungy, got blonde hair down past my nipples. I look like a dangerous lunatic drug addled musician.

I wanna FaceTime Lilli's precious child about trying out for a band situation, this is not going to be easy. I wish I had a chick with me; then all this potential awkweirdness could be averted. I could come back again under the pretense of another chicken buying with a friend girl.

I could talk to Elizabeth all about her 'employment' around the farm. I could transition into a conversation about music and guitar playing. I know, I've got to ask her what was in that case, a strat or a telecaster. Yeah, that's a nonthreatening topic, and to the point, a fairly benign way to initiate contact.

I'm over thinking this and acting like a teen boy asking a girl to the prom; I'm getting all absurd and stuff. I'm not an official talent agent or anything; I don't have a biz card to drop in her lap.

Now I'm wondering, where's her daddy; I could get shot with a double barrel. I hope I don't hear 'CALL 911 NOW!!!' all Skrillex like.

You never know when or where an opportunity may present itself. I mean meeting a female guitar player, a really young female musician is like some kind of solar eclipse, it's rare.

I have done this many times before; but exclusively with male musicians. I've had try-outs with female singers, and they were usually older, more road weary, been around the block a few times. It's a normal part of the business; we're always looking out for prospects, and experiences.

Her mom seems to be a very smart and tough cookie. This 'farm' is a serious deal, and this chick runs all this so she's gotta be tough; and world smart.

Sheeeit, I'm thinking like Humbert Humbert, fixating on the girl and seeing the mom as an obstacle. Maybe Lilli is realistic and grounded and supportive of her daughter's musical career interests. Lilli might just totally wig out when she finds out I want to try-out her naïve, innocent daughter.

Dedicated:

"Thanks" I say to this chicken buying guy; an old Cranberries song is playing in my buds.

Yeah, I think I have a nice singing voice. I wanna put together a band some day; I do play some keyboards too. I probably am going to have to move outta here; somewhere where there are other musicians. I don't know anybody around here or at even school who plays any instruments; except the kids in school band.

My guitar teacher says that I'm blessed with long, strong fingers and that with practice and dedication, I could become very good. He says that every week; 'Dedication' is required for anything; athletes, scientists, anything you want to do and achieve in your life. Its dedication that makes you practice, study, sweat, he's constantly saying.

I think I'm dedicated. I want to get away from this scene way out here; and that desire begets my musical dedication; which begets my hours of practice and playing and singing; Yeah, I am damn dedicated.

I play till my fingers bleed, my nails look like a badger has been gnawing on them; then I sing and play keyboard; after school, alone, for hours; forgoing friendships, lovers, delaying gratification; I am fucking dedicated!

I deliberately let my hair grow freakishly long, it's my moniker. My mom's hair is long, but mine is even longer, past my butt right now. I saw a Stevie Nicks video and she was singing and twirling around with her hair flowing and that inspired me; only mine is really long. Only drawback is I am usually walking around with wet hair because it takes like 2 hours to blow-dry it.

I was thinking how I'm getting a little old for guitar lessons in the mall shop, and I mainly only see little kids with their parents getting lessons. I've gotta find an alternative; what's my next move with this. Actually, I don't freakin know

Chapter 5

Woody's New Cock

Lilli hands me the rooster which I have picked out.

"This guy is probably a year old, so he is sexually mature by now; or soon will be" Lilli explains.

"He reminds me of my old dead friend" I tell Lilli about my beloved rooster and the whole raccoon scenario.

"So Lilli, you ever get any Yokohama breeds?"

"No, what are they?"

"Japanese white chickens. The cocks have these long white tails; I'm mean like 2 feet long, just the tail!"

"Wow, I never saw one."

"Yeah, they are really stunning. You should Wiki it Lilli-san."

As I take the bird and walk towards my truck, I remembered that Cranberries song and how it was recorded in the SD days; I consider recorded music history before HD as the medieval Dark Age. There were no digital devices; people heard music through analog appliances, songs were recorded and played back using tangible physical media necessitating actual human sweat and muscle.

The ingénue is speaking, pointing at my shirt. I think she said she likes D.S.O.T.M. Hmm, now I'm thinking she's a stoner. As I walk closer towards her "I love Pink Floyd," she says, still pointing at my shirt.

Bold move I'm thinking. I am more a Radiohead fan as far as stoner music,

"Me too! Dark Side Of The Moon, Wish You Were Here, The Wall" SMH yes, "Was that like the Cranberries you were singing before?" She nodded yes.

I knew the song because it's a cool song that's been around a while.

"You have an awesome voice; good song too" I told her not knowing if she heard me before.

Thank God it wasn't a Bieber or a 1 D song, I'd sound pretty pervy saying to a teen girl, 'Great song,' if she was singing along with one of those. Now she walks over to the hen house with the bucket of pellets.

Namaste:

I've mostly got what I came here for then I see Elizabeth, finished doing her chores and chilling out, so I steer my path towards her. Ah, I know that song she's singing; *Edge of the Ocean;* cute chick song. I suss out the situation and determine that time is now to talk to her.

I say to Elizabeth "I also liked the bit o' brogue you used in that song."

"Wha "she said.

"That Irish accent, like the girl in the song sings" I said.

"I thought it was British" she said.

"You sound really good; awesome." "I'm Woody," extending my hand to her. My hand is filthy and smells like chickens and nesting crud.

I am not a fan of the hand shake greeting because of germs and such; I'd prefer if our culture would adopt a greeting ritual like, say, the Japanese – people bow to each other. Or something like a fist tap - giving dap. Even better, yoga Namaste.

She takes my handshake; she has long fingers, no nail polish, and no conspicuous ink that I can see. My PEA has supplied me with additional output: If this girl has plans of being some kind of doctor or physicist, or has advanced educational aspirations, she'd cut that hair because to maintain that much hair would take so much time and energy away from academic study time. I mean, isn't it like final exam time around now.

She does menial chores around the farm. I think that Lilli needs her for labor around the farm; more than to be a tiger mom. I'm digging the girl's looks and the vibe she gives off, and of course the strat/tele case she strutted in with, I can also rule out her being a gothic vampiress poser. She's not a hillbilly or 'Deliverance' banjo boy; Relax man, she's just the farmer's daughter with rock n' roll.

She flashes me a serious smile. That smile carried a lot of subliminal information. Again, my PEA is processing: It wasn't a cute shy smile; actually, it was a serious sexy smile and if she were a little older, I'd say she's playin me.

It probably was a "yeah, I know" confident smile, not the former. Jeez, I don't want to 'creep stare' but permanent neural connections are going on in my brain, she's in my head. She impressed me; it's like when you meet a celeb in the flesh.

She's young but hey, I was about 14 when I started gigging; it was brutal, and scary, but a fuck load of fun. That's the way I choose to remember those times.

How many models are discovered by model agents trolling anonymous malls around the earth. All the girls (and guys) that try desperately through normal channels aren't any more likely to be discovered than by some weird alignment of stars and planets; i.e. being at the right place at the right time with the right stuff; that's how life works.

Evolution #9:

1.9 million years ago, homo erectus was sitting in a cave with his friends and family, looking out over the African plain. It isn't raining yet, but the ominous black clouds are pregnant with precipitation. Jagged, forked lightning bolts intermittently grounds the sky with the earth and reports with a deafening thunder clap. Most of his friends and family jam themselves into an alcove near the cave's rear area. One brave and curious fellow does not flee; he watches a flash set a tree on fire. All other creatures are scurrying away into shelters or bolt holes. He runs towards the burning branch, snaps it off and brings it into his cave. He acted against his innate fear and grabbed the fire.

Before long, everyone was using this great, new technology –fire. Probably his wife threw their impala leg onto the fire and BAM the stove was invented. Eating cooked meat required less chewing; our jaw muscles got smaller which left more room in our skulls for the brain to get bigger. Here we are now because somebody took a shot, and successfully grabbed the fire; and used it.

I feel like a pimp; come here for some chickens, now I'm all distracted. I've got my stupid dreams of fame and glory in my head.

I pull out my steampunk mod and start to vape. I felt myself jonesing for a nicotine fix; I had been all preoccupied with this farm and the birds and Lilli and Elizabeth and my dilemma of breaking the ice with her. I need to vape.

Chapter 6

Under the maple tree:

At this point, I decide to join Elizabeth and sit down under the shade of the maple tree. It must be near 90 degrees out today, and I am completely soaked in sweat. There is an arrangement of lawn chairs and chaise lounges under this tree, so I plop down on the chaise.

"Where'd your mom go," I ask Elizabeth.

"Hey," she says while pointing at my neck; "is that a guitar pick?"

I forgot about my cheesy leather choker which I had added 2 guitar picks to go along with the silver crucifix

"Yes, it is a pick" I answer her. "I was wondering, was that a strat or a telecaster in the guitar case I saw you carrying before," I ask because my

Namaste

57

interest in this has been gnawing at me since I first saw the case. Also, I thought, this sort of inside baseball reference would let her know I had some experience with those instruments.

"A Stratocaster" she replied, finally satisfying my curiosity.

Lillian comes over to sit with us, and I beam a sweet smile at her. Gawd, she is a MILF fo sho.

"What you guys talking about" she inquires.

I wait for her daughter to answer. There's an uncomfortable, very pregnant pause before I say "guitars and music Lilli."

"Are you a musician or something Woody" Lilli asks.

"Yes, I am that also" I express enthusiastically in order to elicit a positive vibe from the conversation.

"Elizabeth is a musician too" Lilli expresses with equal enthusiasm.

"Mom" Elizabeth states with that obvious contemptuous, impatience that most teen daughters have for their mothers. The word starts off with a 'MMMMM' in a mono pitch tone, then transitions into the emphasis on the 'o' by stretching it out and modulating the pitch up and down one note step, then fading out the final 'mmmm...'. It was beautiful, a song itself.

Then it hit me; by Lilli volunteering that information about Elizabeth, it conveyed two pieces of data: first, if Lilli categorizes and considers her daughter a musician, that means she is in support of promoting her; and secondly, she is in favor and enthusiastically wants me to continue this conversation with her.

My brain PEA is impressive; at least I think so. "So you play the guitar Elizabeth" I query although I already know this.

"Yeah, I've been playing for like two years. So I'm not that good yet" she adds. She tells me about some songs she has learned to play.

"I've been playing for like 15 years, so I'm not that good yet also" I hoped she'd understand that humor for the purpose of loosening the mood. Both Lilli and Elizabeth respond with a smile and an affirmative giggle; so cute.

"My friends call me E" Elizabeth explains.

"I like that, E" I eagerly respond back. She is basically friending me at this point; that's what I determine. She sounds so serious through the whole conversation, so mature.

"Are you a musician also" I ask Lilli.

"Ha. Nooo. She's a spaz!" Elizabeth snaps for her mother.

That would be awesome if she was. "Well Lilli, let's settle up; what do I owe ya" I ask as I pull out my cash.

"Let's see: 4 reds; 2 whites; and the cock; and the 2 barred rocks – ninety dollars will be good," Lilli stated.

"Okay, I got a hundy" I hand her the bill.

As she starts apparently rummaging through her pockets for a ten for change I tell her "Oh forget it Lillian, I had such a nice tour man!"

Flying the Coop:

I realized that my birds were cooped up on this hot day and that I should get going. I look through my pockets for a piece of paper and found none so I grab my pen and walk over to the brown bag of

Namaste

cracked corn. On it I write out my contact information for FaceTime and/or texting.

"Let's discuss some sort of try out in like a studio situation" I tell the girls.

I continue with my plan, "We'll learn some tunes we mutually agree to, songs which you can play or sing. If it works out, then we can consider some sort of collaboration or you can play me things you are working on."

"Where are you gonna do this try-out" Lilli asks.

Of course the mom is gonna be nervous about this phase so I come up with a safe compromise.

"Well, I can send her some mp3s to practice, then we can pick a time when it's convenient for you two to come over to my studio. I'll have the band mates, and we can jam; we would be trying out each other."

At this time both Lilli and Elizabeth name some songs that Elizabeth knows, both how to sing and the guitar parts to.

"I'd really like to see if you can, you know, front a band."

Lilli asks "What is that, front a band."

"Which song do you think you could sing best, *Believe* by Cher or *Magic Man* by Heart" I asked mainly to set the bar high and see how she responds.

"Wow, those songs are something Woody," Lilli adds sounding a little choked up.

"Those songs are like total opposites Woody" Elizabeth shoots back.

I was impressed with the fact that she even knew the songs, never mind how different they were from each other.

"Just wanted to see what song you see yourself doing; something auto-tune and disco or something heavy phase guitar and rock." I explain to them, and then add "that's okay, Elizabeth, you think about it and you pick out what you like, pick out only what you want to do."

"When you front, it's your show, your band. You probably have already dreamed of yourself performing. You've imagined yourself doing certain songs, having a certain sound, having a certain look, in your mind's scenario; am I right Elizabeth? All of us musicians do that; especially when we're young," I explained a rather long-winded, but important point; which I knew Elizabeth would dig.

I tried to stress to her that she would have to be assertive and be confident in what she was singing and playing. I then explain, briefly, about some of the tunes I have constructed and recorded which I imagined could be 'chick-a-fied.'

"Ultimately, I'd like for us to co-author a couple three songs which we can demo," I explain mainly for Lillian's sake.

Plan 9:

I briefly map out the strategy to the girls:

- ❖ write some songs
- ❖ record the demo
- ❖ shop it around. That should not take more than a month, 2 at the most for like 3 or 4 songs. If someone digs it; some A&R person, some agent; then,
- ❖ we get fronted to go to a professional recording studio with professional engineers and with a Z of blow and bang out like a dozen tunes.

"And that, girlfriend, is basically it; that's the business plan; e z p z, nice and easy; or, we post the demo on kickstarter and fund an album."

Namaste

Gapping silence ensues so I explain "You know I jest with y'all about the blow thing, aight."

I immediately started freaking myself out fearful that I just screwed things up with that drug reference.

Elizabeth is giggling and says "Wow, you dug yourself in deep Woody."

"I couldn't stop myself; I say inappropriate things at times, sorry." I say as I feel myself getting extra sweaty again.

"I use sarcasm to relieve tension. Well, on that note, I gotta bolt ladies. Those girls and I got a long drive home."

"Sayonara, Lilli-san, Lizzy-san," the girls giggle and we exchange handshakes and good-byes.

Veni, Vidi, Vici:

I came here; saw some spectacular birds; bought them. Best of all, I've vidi a smokin hottie babe, she might be unattached – no ring, and she gave me her number. I got her even prettier daughter's number also; although, that's business.

All in all, I'd say this turned out to be a very prosperous endeavor after all. I might wind up with a girlfriend and a chick front man all in one convenient drive thru.

I thought how we spent about an hour under that tree; Lilli spoke ardently about Elizabeth's music career desires. I am impressed with this guitar girl; she has important characteristics like self-motivation, and discipline; reminds of me at that age. I drove myself to my guitar lessons and paid for them with my paper route money; along with all my guitars, music, and sheet music.

Didn't need my parents telling me to practice; I enjoyed playing so much I did it myself.

During the drive home, I was so stoked. If this chick is as good as I hope she is, this is gonna be great. Wish I uploaded some demo mp3s I had recorded of potential girl-able tunes. They are playing in my mind's ipod as I drive. If she can compose, wow even greater. I mean even if she's not gig ready right now, she might be studio ready – that's even better.

I also kept remembering her mom's enthusiasm for her daughter's musical calling. I've never seen a parent so supportive of their child getting involved in such a notoriously skeevy industry such as the music profession. She even made sure I had both her and her girl's numbers. It must be nice to have your parents so supportive of your wild and crazy dreams. Especially by such a level headed and obvy smart woman like Lilli. Jeez, my parents could give a fuck about my music; they could give a fuck if we even had food in the house.

Elizabeth Ponders Woody:

I think I came off very stiff to Woody. I tried to smile nicely at him, I think I looked weird. I tried to be all flirty and cute. I probably came off as retarded. I can't do goofy. That's like not in my genetics. I know even some of my closest friends can do the whole goofy shit around boys; It gets results. I can't even fake it; can't, not even if my life depended on it. My girlfriends can do goofy so smooth; they have alternates in them so it's easy. My mind intercepts me when I attempt goofy; comes off as just plain stupid; that's not me. I've put a lot of time into my music and probably wasn't there when the how to bring up your goofy alter was taught; now I'm socially awkward.

My mind was flooded with all the possibilities, all the plans that Woody had talked to me about. I hope this guy is for real and shit. I was thinking about how he said I've got to aspire to a particular sound and a look; a style.

I went in my room and did a Wikipedia search of all the girls I can think of who started their music careers and were successful at around my age:

1) Christina Aguilera
2) Avril Lavigne
3) Kelly Rowland
4) Beyoncé
5) Pink
6) Lorde

Omigod, I could go on for like a long list here. I feel like I gotta get my career going now, I'm getting old fast.

I thought about Woody saying how we dream of performances; how I would sound, and how I would look.   Then I was thinking how my mom says I look like Brigitte Bardot, when she was like 16; especially when I put all my hair up in a sorta beehive bun and still have a bunch of hair hanging down; you mean like a blonde Amy Winehouse I'd explain to her.

I guess I have been trying to have a look, a style; like all artists have.   I am so excited for when he calls, hope soon; can't wait to get this thing going.

Chapter 7

Face Timing:

"I forgot to ask you but how old are you E?"

"I'm gonna be 15 in two months" she said.

"Wow, I thought that you were like around 16, going on 17 or 18; so you're actually 14, wow."

"Why, does that creep you up," she asks.

"I overestimated, a bit." I laughed uncomfortably.

"Wow, you won't even be old enough to vote in the next presidential election, will ya?"

"If I was, I'd vote for Hillary"

"Why?"

"Girlpower."

"Well remember, the last pharaoh of Egypt was female, and she wound up being paraded through Rome as spoils." I just had to swing at that.

I explained to her that I was about 12-ish when I started playing, and was around 14 when I started my first band and played gigs; doing air quotes when saying gigs; expounding on the whole high school party gigs thing and how much fun that was. We talked about the kinds of music we liked, and I started thinking of my presupposition of why she's not into age/gender appropriate music.

"My favorite Pandora station is 90's Alternative/Grunge" she explained. "I grew up listening to all that stuff."

"My dad has a lot of fake books and sheet music for those songs."

She goes on about her dad's rock n' roll younger days and how he use to gig and now he's 45 and works from home.

Namaste

"A really sad story sweetheart, and now he lives with you and the ball and chain," I ask somewhat disappointed.

I didn't know if Lilli was attached or not; and was crestfallen to have my suspicions confirmed.

"How old is your mom?"

"Why, you like her or something?"

"She seems very nice Elizabeth. Just that she looks my age but she can't be cause then she would have to have you at like 12."

"She's gonna be 31 soon, she had me when she was 15."

"Your dad's 15 years older. Was your mom a runaway?"

"Can we change the subject Woody?"

"Sure. There is one more thing which is very serious that we need to get out of the way A-S-A-

P" I explain to E in a somber tone, adding a nice touch of anxiety to the conversation.

"What is it" she replies apprehensively.

"Well, I might as well just spit it out...You DO know you are gonna to have sex with me; and then the rest of the band. It's the standard way of jumping in to a band!"

After what seemed to be like a cone of silence descending over her, "Wha" is what she could spit out after what felt like a 10 minute guzzle from her bottle of water.

I then explained to her about my theory on band m8s sexual tensions and distractions; how bands disintegrate due to this unresolved tension; and how we could collaborate more efficiently and be more productive if we can resolve this issue pronto.

Namaste

I presented my argument seriously and with a sense of a call to duty.

"Really?" was her simple, yet impactful statement.

"Look, you're the one who wanted to change the subject when I asked about your mom. You really got like all tense and distorted when I asked about her; I sense something underlying there."

"I told you that humor and sarcasm are coping mechanisms of mine. Why do you have to be so annoyed with me; you seem ticked off much of the time; typical Viking girl."

"I'm Dutch!" she explained

"Erikson is Viking, Dutch are Viking, same difference as Nordics."

"Do you know about your lineage?"

"What like my grandparents and stuff?"

"Or even further back?"

"You're a Viking because those people, the Norwegians, probably raided some costal Dutch village in like 933AD; they raped the women, plundered the village, killed all the men; some liked the place and stayed. Some Viking guy hooked up with some Dutch girl because, remember there were no men left. That is your genetics, those are your great- greats. That's basically your DNA baby girl"

"You carry the most famous Viking name – Erickson, come on!"

"I have papers and docs from the government and the church going back over 200 years on my line; Germany and Ireland."

"My great grandfather left Germany when he was 18 and came to the Bronx. My great grandmother left Ireland when she was 14 and met my ggf and married a year later. I always wonder how they communicated. She spoke English but he was German, how'd they court?"

"Yeah Woody, that's mysterious."

"That wasn't so weird in those days; I guess."

"I wanna look up my stuff like that Woody."

"You might find some strange characters in your lineage, be forewarned."

"What, like a Hitler person?"

"Exactly. Or royalty."

"E, you got to have balls" I blurted out to her "Balls of steel, stones of depleted uranium oxide."

"What the hell you talking about," she says sounding all jumbled.

I explain, "I remember when I was young seeing Hole in concert. Right off the bat, she comes out and kicks over a speaker, hocks a loogie into the crowd, starts singing; I was young, but it was a cool performance, and she didn't seem that drunk. I think that's who it was."

"All that cool music you listen to, I seen half those bands live."

"I wish you could've seen those guys in their prime, they had balls – even the chicks!" I explained to her that my step-brother was older than me; I tagged along with him and his friends and got to go to tons of shows.

"Capeesh" I ask her.

We must have talked for nearly 6 hours. Sometime along the way we wound up picking up our guitars and doing some FTime tele-jamming. She showed me around her room, her audio/video system. She showed me her Fender Stratocaster; a sweet blackie with a maple neck.

"Ooo, that amp is new, right?" as she showed her acoustic and her amp, which was a cool Spider IV amp; the big one.

"Yeah it is new."

"It has all the effects and modeling. Do you have the cool foot pedal with all the controls?"

"Mine just clicks up and down."

"I have that amp, I love it. I also got the big foot controller for it."

I showed her around my modest studio and all my guitars and amps. I show her the percussion room; the vocals iso booth; the control room with all the computer monitors; the various outboard signal processors; the cable rack; speaker monitors; the mixer board.

"Ever seen or used Pro Tools."

"No, what are they?"

"A DAW; that's the software package used for recording everything; it also processes and master's the tracks. Once you learn it, you can pretty much record anything anyway you want."

She described to me her jamming with her guitar teacher. I told her how, in college, I played in a madrigal guitar ensemble – and exactly what that is.

"I like to write a lot at night. I'll wake up in the middle of the night and maybe because of a dream or just an idea for a song will be in my head. So I'll write it down the best I can. How about you Woody?"

"We're sharing a brain baby doll. I do a lot of my stuff at night also. That's why I always have my laptop with my DAW software on in case I wanna bang out some song. I have learned to never let an inspiration wait till later because I always lose it; like some Higgs Boson particle, puff, it's gone."

Namaste

I can't believe she left that whole sex talk proposition just hanging. She had no further comments about the subject, and I forgot to close that loop. Now, I'm completely distracted. My sarcasm had backfired; it's fucking around with my head.

Excited E:

After that jamming conversation session with Woody, I'm exhausted. I'm shot full of excitement anticipating getting together with him in person, and jamming. I lay on my bed completely flooded with thoughts and ideas, totally motivated, my head buzzing like my fingers. I am absolutely enamored with him. I can't wait to show him what I got. It feels so good to be recognized as a professional musician, to be taken seriously by someone who has been around, someone who knows.

I've got to get my mom to stop peeping in on my conversations with Woody; it causes me to hold things back, to be all self-critical. I know she does it because she digs him. Woody and I have a loose and unrestricted relationship so it promotes our imaginations when we are collaborating.

Just the other day Woody and I were working on a song; I was singing the lyrics to a song we were trying to write; the words were generally about this girl getting dumped by her great lover for a major slut. There was drinking and fighting and name calling; bottom line, the girl was godsmacked and heartbusted. My mom was lurking about and overheard my stuff; she practically dialed 911; she didn't understand it was just lyrics; doesn't appreciate the process.

Mom gets all uneasy about themes Woody and I banter about with each other. Like she's freaking out because I told him about how dad grows those marijuana plants and how my p's are major blazers. Take a chill pill; Woody is so 420 ok.

The Other Shoe:

"What's going on E" Pepper answers her phone.

"You on speaker Pepper?"

"Not now, what's up?"

"I'm gonna be working with Woody next weekend."

"Oh shit E. You're blowing off Carlos and Us and Great Adventure for that!"

Pepper realized how insensitive that was to say immediately.

"I'm sorry E, I know how important your music is to you. Are you sure that that guy isn't saying he likes your music and shit just to get in your pants?"

"So you're saying that I'm a naive hick or something."

"Come on Elizabeth, I didn't think that. I'm just, well he's so much older and you don't know him. I just feel like you're disappearing into a black hole or something."

"First of all P, I've been working with Woody enough times to know him as well as most of our friends know their boyfriends before they're giving them blow jobs. If he wanted just to get into my pants, this is the most convoluted seduction I've ever heard of."

"I didn't mean it that way Elizabeth."

"Ima go now, my head's killing I. I&i Pepper."

"I&i. That's cool. I love you E."

Pepper and I used be into this whole Rastafari thing; had a special vocabulary and accent; dreadlock talk mon.

Wow, it seems as though I ain't got nobody. I have no friends.

Why can't anybody just be happy for me. I'm a good girl. I'm trying to do something that I believe will be a career. My wires are crossed or something; my head is killing me.

Boy Problems:

Lately, I'm having major boy troubles. More like Carlos trouble. Carlos is mad at me. I said this would happen, eventually. He's having a total meltdown over me spending so much time with Woody. I guess I can't blame the guy; I hardly speak to him anymore. Ever since Woody, I have been spending even more time practicing and now composing. Plus the time I spend with Woody, I haven't done anything with Carlos, or Pepper, or anyone.

Right in the middle of a long phone conversation with Carlos, bang, I became aware. My phone was hot, my ear was numb; then, an ice pick of truth impaled itself into my membrane. Wrenched me out of a nice run of romantic baby talk dialogue I was having with Carlos. I then became fluent in speaking blunt. I proceeded then to lay my cards on the table, show my hand. Wow, I didn't just burn bridges; I nuked and salted the earth.

"Carlos," I snapped. "I believe you are satisfied being stuck here. My future is with Woody."

"Ew, he is so old Elizabeth. He's like a pervy dude who is manipulating you E."

"That's not true at all Carlos; he isn't taking me anywhere I didn't already want to go."

"Where's that Elizabeth, where are you gonna go?"

"Carlos, I envisioned the path before me. I envisioned myself, my dream, my music, Woody. You're not there, you're not coming along. Where is Carlos?…certainly, not with me."

I have to cut this boy loose. I have to let him turn on a separate path, a new direction. It wouldn't include me.

"Carlos, I actually have to tell you that it's not you - it's me; no really, it's me."

"I really mean that. There's nothing wrong with you. We are at that age…" I tried to smooth things out with glib platitudes when he shot back;

"Talk about age, you're really fucking stupid about this guy. He's telling you anything you want to hear. You are gonna wind up disappearing, chained up in his basement, impregnated."

"You think he's lying to me. Telling me I have talents, I have a gift, just so he can fuck me?"

"Damn it Elizabeth, you don't understand men. Guys like that are creepy and will figure out what you wanna hear; what will get you excited. They read your body language; they figure out if you're desperate for parental affection and shit. You tell him about the problems with your dad, and he becomes the nice father that you desire. He'll use your weaknesses to control you."

"You're saying he's exploiting my vulnerabilities from being traumatized?"

"This is not a joke, he's playing you Elizabeth and I'm really worried."

"Are all the bros and hoes talking the same; y'all think this?" I say emotionless.

"Yeah, we're all worried about you; bros, hoes!"

"Pepper too?" I ask, even more crestfallen.

"Hmm, so Carlos, you're saying I'm just a hack who is so ditzy and I'm using my vagina to get ahead? Do you realize that that is pretty much the most insensitive meanest thing a person can say?"

"I have never told Woody anything about my father; the only way you know is because of Pepper's big mouth. We have a very businesslike relationship – so far; but you're probably thinking all perverted stuff."

"What do you mean? *so far*?" Carlos stresses.

"I'm happy when I'm with him; I like feeling happy – finally."

"Wow, it's good to have such friends as you, and Pepper" I intonate sarcastically.

"Just think Carlos, in 3 months when you turn 18, you'll technically be an adult; you'll be the child rapist, the sexual predator if we had sex, right; or even inappropriate touching of a minor?"

"You're really just being a jealous hypocrite; it's not the age difference that's bugging you, it's that he's a guy, who I show some interest in."

"You're taking this all wrong; you're not getting it E. He is a lot older."

"Carlos, you're the one citing the statutory rape code. The law is the law and you'd be an adult, while I'm still a minor."

"You don't know Woody so you're lashing out, and that's natural. I haven't been a good girlfriend anyway. You probably expected sex with me by now. We don't spend time together; we don't have many common interests, common friends. I don't watch you play that often, you don't watch me; so you can do better."

"Is Pepper worried about this too? You two talked about the *E matter*?"

"Well of course, she's really worried. She wants me and her to go and kill this fucking guy."

"Ha, that's so freaking funny; you guys."

"I am basically dumping you for another guy Carlos; and you should be pissed; you should be murderous. I'm worth murdering for; at least Woody thinks so."

"I guess I'm going in a different direction babe. Pepper is a sweet girl; why not ask her out, I know she isn't into Peter that much. She likes going with him when she can go out with us," I throw in out of character.

"So this is it Elizabeth. I am still gonna worry about you and this guy. He's playing you and if he hurts you, I'm gonna hurt him."

"I know he'd never say that mean thing that you said to me before, never."

"I'm sorry, it didn't come out right. It's kinda hard for me to compete with a faker."

"Again Carlos; if he's a faker that means I'm a stupid, gullible dork."

"I appreciate all your concern. I'll be okay; really. I'll talk to all y'all later. If you don't hear from me for a while, come looking in Woody's basement; unless of course, you see it on the local hysterical news channel first." I make a kiss kiss sound and hang up.

The thing that's most painful is not their ridiculousness, but the fact that they feel it would be inconceivable that someone would see a unique talent in me. I'm not gonna let them bring me down. I'm not gonna let all them deter me like my father always does. As a matter of fact, I'm more motivated to do anything and everything I gotta do to get the fuck outta here.

"O baby, I'm so sorry they hurt you like that" my mom says as she walks into my room. She evidentially was eavesdropping again.

"Mom, why do you have to hover like that? I am hurt; betrayed. That was a pretty harsh conversation."

"If you want privacy, you shouldn't leave your door open." She defends herself.

I slam the door shut. I'm thinking how her presence makes me feel like my thoughts are trapped in some sticky thick goo. Sometimes the sound of my internal voice of her voice grates the bones of my ears, sending the sound vibrating into my skull.

She has a way of dousing any creative sparks along with any emotional warmth I try to feel. It's not her fault; the way I get embarrassed in front of her. She brings out the way I unleash my particular harsh judgment of my own inspiration.

She's overcompensating for her own guilt; because of my father's treatment of me; because she begged him back into our lives, because she got pregnant so young – by him.

I know she's still checking this guy out, looking out for me. She tries to be a good mom and all, but she can get all obnoxious.

There is this pall hanging over every interaction between my mother and me; between my dad and me. Every wave of sound; every photon and molecule has to pass through the membrane of this matter; it's the whole age thing projected again through spacetime; isn't it ironic.

Because she had me at the age she did; because my dad was 15 years older; technically a major; adjudicated a minor. Did she have to deal with best frenemies who disappointed her like mine.

I know my dad is disappointed that I choose to spend time with Woody and not Carlos. I know he thinks that I'm screwing up like he and mom did; her falling for an older, musician guy, eventually leading to a positive pregnancy pee stick. He doesn't get it, I'm the musician in this, not just a junkie groupie.

My dad thinks I'm blowing my opportunity to have the big sports hero; the star quarterback. He sees his whole life as a bunch of mistakes and repair jobs on those mistakes. He and mom used to go to AA or NA meetings, and go to church all the time when I was young. They were both heroin users. Now I've got to live my life as an example; I've got to be clean of any mistakes. If you have no mistakes in your life, it means you didn't do anything. An error free life; who has that? I'm not gonna live in fear of errors; dreading slip-ups.

I'm afraid that my dad is jealous of Woody. He's pissed off at the time I spend with him and the band, he's pissed that all I talk about is music; he's jealous that I have no energy or time for quote, the family, close quote. I truly hope things don't get nasty or violent. That's why I can't tell Woody everything about my home situation.

I wonder if Woody is aware that the list of his enemies is building: Carlos, Pepper, and my Dad; in fact, the only supporters he has around this freaking hillbilly town are my mom and I.

Amped Head Case:

"Heyyyee baby doll, wassup in da 2-0-1," I'm singing a song that I know irritates her when I call Elizabeth.

"Hi, that's hilarious, not" she expresses contemptibly.

"Oi vay! Somebody on the rag or something," I say in an exasperated tone.

"Naw, I'm dealing with a headache again, I'm sorry" she says with a sad puppy-dog expression.

"Aww, I know all about that deal sweetie. Do you want me to come over and help you with that?" I commiserate with her.

"Wait…..What! You can't come all the way over here just because I have a stupid headache."

"Of course I would. You've never had someone, a guy; really care about you, have you? Well, that's what good guys do for the women we care about."

I had once told her my personal head history. I have had terrible migraines my whole life. When I was a child, I used to get so sick with them, I would be sweating and shaking, I would puke and heave. I still get them but not as often as a child, I'd get them every month, sometimes twice a month. Now I just use my headache cocktail which is comprised of some serious narcotics and about 4 – 6 Advil Liquid GelCaps with maybe 3 or 4 cups of coffee and a benzo if I have any.

I told Elizabeth about my headache cocktail and she tells me hers, which is similar, minus the coffee. I tell her how the caffeine is a key ingredient.

"Remember that tantra yoga stuff we did?"

"Yeah, that really helped. But Woody, you are not here."

"Well, imagine we're doing that. Remember big bang expansion and singularity. I place my hands on your temples; I slowly am stroking your head. Your breathing; be aware of your breath, slow it down, in the nose, out the mouth. Your heartbeat; be aware of your heart; as you breathe slower and deeper, your heart beats slower. You can feel my hands pushing the tension, pushing the pain down the sides of your head and with each breath, you blow out more and more of the tension and stress…"

"Dasa anu dasa." Elizabeth says in a trance monotone breathy voice.

I keep talking and trail my voice off with each mantra.

About 5 minutes of silence, except for her slowed deep breath.

"Okay baby doll, I'll let you go and deal. Contact me when you feel better. And I would definitely drive over there if you need me."

"I'm sorry Woody; I'll be okay later and call ya. That helped even though you're not right here."

"Hi Lilli, how ya been" I ask her mom when I see her come into view of the webcam.

"Oh, hey there Woody, I'm doing good, I've gotta deal with our girl here" Lilli explains with that concerned mommy voice.

Namaste

"Aww, I know. O-Tay hit me up later, aight, byeeee bitches" waving at the camera as I respond with baby talk expressions to sound all cute and concerned. Poor baby girl.

I really dig Lilli. She's a major hottie herself, but I am amazed by her acceptance of her daughter's musical vocation. She understands that Elizabeth is sui generis. Most parents don't get it – young artists have to be given license to be expressive in their own, distinctive ways; Elizabeth's lucky that her mom is cool – I'm glad she's hot.

Chapter 8

Cray Cray E:

Elizabeth is at my house, we are working alone in the studio. The other times we got together here, we had the band m8s for some rehearsing. I tell Elizabeth how impressed they are with her, especially her singing; they really think she sounded great and could probably develop a stage presence with the right material.

"The fuck do they know; those guys are like technicians and it's gotta be right in front of them. They can't envisage it," I told her.

This time we thought we just want to compose stuff and put down some basic tracks. We can get more work done right now alone. Elizabeth, like so many noobies, is falling in love with double tracking and the compressor on her vocal tracks.

Anyway, it looks like her and Christina, my bass player's wife, hit it off. Tina is a sweet, great looking babe. She's got beautiful long black hair, and a killer bod.

"Tina tell you she is a school teacher?"

"Yes. She and Jerry been married for nearly ten years; she is so young." Elizabeth said questioningly.

"I guess. She looks like a college student, but she's like 26 now. She met Jerry in college."

"Wait. What. How's that work out."

"She started college at like 17. She's really smart. They met upstate; she was a student and he was gigging with his band; same band he's still with now."

"Tina's parents own a pawn store in Queens. I've gotten quite a few instruments and equipment from them, for a good deal."

"Anyway, you look like you're tired or crying, everything okay" I asked Elizabeth; but it looked like I opened a can of worms with that statement because she had a breakdown and I had to work hard to keep her from psychoing out.

"I would like her to stay outta my business," she expressed all emotional.

"Who, your mom again?"

"You know that you are really fortunate that your mom is cool with all this" I tell Elizabeth after a lengthy bitch session she laid on me complaining about her mom.

"Is she hovering all up in your bidness? Newsflash, that's what moms do. I think you're overreacting."

"She's like the helicopter from hell," Elizabeth had that low gravelly tone.

"You know what else I think" I say and let enough time pass to hear if she objected to me continuing.

"I think Lilli is all into you getting into the music business because she is really attracted to musicians."

Again, I wait for her response, then continue, "She hooked up with your dad when he was a musician; she was attracted to all that," I pause for a response.

"She likes me. She was very encouraging when I asked to try you out. She trusts me with you," I continue on.

"Your mom wants to see you succeed in this; your mom is basically a groupie, a fangirl."

Elizabeth, finally, with stunned realization adds "I know, I know.   And I really appreciate her enthusiasm."

"You know this is not the sort of thing she can help me with. I'm trying to write songs, I'm trying to write and practice music, she can't help with that. I work with you, she's not a songwriter."

I tell Elizabeth "You got to explain stuff to her. Include her when you can; tell her to back off when you need."

"Comprende, capeesh, understand," and I hope my counseling duties are complete; homicide averted.

"You know in this business, or basically any endeavor where one has to present to the public songs or stories that you have created causes a lot of stress; a fear," I explain to Elizabeth.

"You mean because you put yourself out there through your music," Elizabeth asks.

"You put yourself out there to be judged. Here it is, like it or not!" I add.

"I try not to think about that aspect of song creating Woody."

"Whatever works baby girl. I tell myself that I should be more afraid of not putting my stuff out there, and my stuff is really good. That's worse because you've denied yourself and the people of some stuff that might be greatly appreciated; you know what I mean Elizabeth?"

"Um, yeah that's a tortuous way of looking at it. Like you said, whatever works?"

I've got to remember how much of a drama queen scene teen girls can display. The irrational hostility that that girl has towards her mom; she had the veins in her neck popping; I had to remember that it's a natural struggle between mothers and their teen daughters. I had to explain to her that time will heal the mother daughter schism; in other words, she'll grow up and get tired of fighting with Lilli, and Lilli will appreciate her girl; or not.

Jeez, that girl has a lot of frustration built up in her. Maybe that's the source of her headaches; but that anger comes out in her gift too. I don't want to screw around with that. I love her anger, she does channel it. I can't wait until we start gigging live; wow, that girl might have the stones to perform after all. Her rage in a convoluted way makes her happy.

Out of the Frying Pan:

I think we wrote a couple of really good songs the other night. Elizabeth was definitely in touch with her emotions and pouring out her soul in some quality heartfelt lyrics; and some interesting compelling verses.

We were certainly channeling our inner Lennon-McCartney; or Jagger-Richards; or more like Goffin-King.

One thing about that anger of hers is someday she's going to turn it on me. I know this because band situations are like an intense hyper-marriage. You're with each other for hours and hours, day after day. You're working together under sometimes extremely stressful sometimes gruelingly monotonous situations. Many times there is drug and alcohol use and abuse. Anger always rears up; and Elizabeth already has an anger thing.

Girls like that, getting all pissed off and foaming at the mouth is so cute; until she stabs me or throws a hammer at me – she definitely is a potential accidental murderer; I gotta keep the sharp stuff away. She's gonna have to learn some anger coping skills someday or that head pain will manifest as a cancerous tumor somewhere.

Namaste

Into the Fire:

I am stressing out how that psychodrama about her mother resolved the other night. Although Elizabeth is not into PDA; crying is a display of her aggravation. The irrational frustration manifests itself deep inside her soul only to betray her struggle to appear like a colossus, floating above all the emotional affect. It was a deeply affectionate outburst, especially for a girl like Elizabeth. I know she holds a lot of what's inside her, deep inside; she keeps a lot of what's outside her, far outside. I know even the anger she does display is tempered. I fear she's going to dissolve in her own stomach acid one day. Whatever experiences had marred her, now expresses out her eyes, streaking down her cheeks, and finally into her mouth.

That was the night I became very aware of how I was falling for her; and it was revealed she felt the same about me. All that emotional rawness inevitably led her to tears; tears out of utter frustration. At first I took a Kleenex and wiped her tears. I wasn't going to bring up the subject, I would let it flow from her organically, but I suspected that her anger at her mom was displaced. Her real target I suspected, was her dad. There's something off with the guy and I fear just how off he may be.

Never made sense to me all that venom aimed at her mother. More likely, mom is useless to fix whatever is wrong so Elizabeth's frustration gets vented at her.

Later on, at some point we engaged in some innocent hugging for encouragement; you know, for support and suddenly it all became sensual and romantic. I innocuously kissed the salty droplets from her wet face. Elizabeth being so nice and tall made it convenient to stare deeply into those awesome leopard-like green eyes. Flashing that alluring leer; like when we first met at her farm that day I was buying birds; and it is now what I thought it was then.

We stood there, in each other's arms; comforting her stress which had me fixated into a longer and deeper gaze into her pretty emerald eyes; I now notice every eye speckle, and the length and thickness of her lashes. She batted them at me penetrating into my blues, the enigmatic flashing code of love; unforeseen and subliminal.

I felt as though we were standing on a centrifuge table, with her completely in focus, and behind her the scene rotated in high speed blur behind her. The room was literally spinning, but not me, and not her.

All that electricity evoked a magnetic embrace with her head fitted into my chest and tucked aptly under my chin. She stroked her fingers along the backs of my encompassing arms and a shivering followed her strokes as she swiped her fingers along my spine.

She stared up into my eyes, traced down my face to my mouth, inviting my lips to complete the circuit. I kissed the top of her head, managing my hands down her back and let them come to rest on the small of her back; restraining my fingers from sliding inside, confining my hands to pressing her cheeks outside her jeans.

I flared up with an overpowering intensity, and then thought *aw fuck it*, and plunged my hands down inside her jeans. I cupped her cheeks digging my fingers into her soft skin, and drew her up snug, and into me, partially raising her off her heels. The circuit was complete when my lips pressed firmly on her mouth, our tongues introducing themselves to each other.

Disconnecting the kiss far enough so she would gaze into my eyes, and then reconnecting again.

I found myself continuously checking into her eyes to get a measure on how far I could take this. With the language of her eyes, she pleads for me to grab her harder, to go further, to do more. She registered a silent appeal from the tip of her tongue, to the cusp of her breath to go over the edge; to experience something she had never known resided within her. I wanted her, she wanted me, we were gonna do this proper; no regrets.

I hoisted her up completely now, walking in reverse, never losing contact with her mouth and her look. Somehow we floated onto the bed, initially with me on top, flipping over placing her on top and symbolically in control. Simultaneously the swirling concoction of sex hormones flooding our bodies, which were preparing it for ecstasy, and the taboo nature of

Namaste

this impending felony, I feared I would not be able to summon up the will to resist.

Her dilated pupils were resolving from the emerald jewel of her gaze, into the black on black stare of a stalking predator. I felt her heart like detonations; her savage breathing like rapid hot gasps. Her sweat soaked face had obliterated evidence of tear streaks; her hair sticking across her cheeks and forehead. Our sweating bodies prompted spontaneous unbuttoning, crazed rending of clothes; the truth being that we were quite overdressed for this moment.

"What time is it Elizabeth?"

"Oh please," she says in anguished frustration because I snap us into reality.

She presses down on me with her weight. Despite retaining my jeans; through her panties, I feel her white hot incision grinding on my trunk.

I remove my hands from her back and plop them along my side.

"Woody."

"Please!" Her submissiveness becomes despair.

"Don't. Just a little more," she begs me as she continues to contort her body over me.

I feel her go limp, faints from forgetting to breathe; she revives with a feral grin and gasps "Oh baby, oh boy!"

It took nothing short of praying to God to deliver me from temptation to be able to grasp my phone and then respond to my own question with "looks like 2am. We got to get you home baby girl."

"Don't stop. Not now. Woody. Please!"

"You know I'm all fucked up in the head over this Elizabeth, now I can't."

I think she fainted.

She breathes, as though she had forgotten to, all this time.

"I'm too shot to go all the way home. Okay I stay here?" she stated while grabbing my phone.

Elizabeth then called her mom to explain that we were all dialed in on a creative roll and we didn't want to stop working, so she would sleep at my house and I'd drive her back home the following afternoon. She bid her mom goodnight and turned out the light then plopped down beside me. I lifted the comforter up and we scooched under the covers; I lay on my back staring up at the ceiling, she on her side with her arm draped over me and her head on my arm. As our sweat evaporated into dreams the raging desires subside, we kiss.

"You understand why I can't babe?"

"Yes. That was so nice," she expressed with frustration.

I thought of how her mom was probably having flashbacks after receiving that call that evening, about the night a 15 year old fangirl spent being deflowered by an older musician guy, and how now history may be repeating itself. How she may be wondering if there is some special planetary alignment, say Venus at a particular point in the eastern sky, repeating on that night and this night. Should I ask Elizabeth exactly how Lilli said the words affirming that she could spend the night with me? Ultimately, I'm left pondering, are Lilli's flashbacks romantic, or traumatic.

Sex with band m8s is as treacherous as sex with office m8s. Throw in the odd personality disorders which are musicians; male or female. Perhaps we at the least might get some new lyric material from it all.

I think she was buzzed; I know I was. I'm usually immune to strong narcs because I have been using them on and off for so many years, I've developed quite a tolerance; but that purple lean the m8s brought over was sneaky. Sprite and sizzurp; whatever, it kicked my ass. She seemed fairly okay so I doubt she had any. Now I've got to deal; got to call to see if we have a problem; all that drama and shredding of clothes; all that tension; my head is now throbbing.

Reality; it is my mind's best guess that what my mind is rendering is actually real. I would put myself into a metaphysical loop to induce a transcendental tranquility; until my meds take effect; and I resolve Elizabeth. Yeah, I'm overthinking this.

I noticed occasionally, the tiny thought would creep into my consciousness; where was her daddy in all this. Why isn't he interested in his daughter's business; why isn't he checking me out? I know me, I know that I am a good guy, but he doesn't know shit about me and she's worth fighting for. I also notice myself repressing these

Namaste

thoughts about her father because I fear I'll jump to a conclusion which will freak me out. I might transform into a raging man slaughterer; justified or not. Am I bad for not pressing the issue? No doubt, she will tell me what's up someday; I'm just trying to gird myself for the most horrendous so that I say and act rationally; that's what she'll need.

O man, the m8s big wig out over the first time I showed them one of Elizabeth's songs she titled *Running a Hole in the Wind.* I show them the tab sheet first because I knew they would see it as a simple, girlie song. I had to explain how it wasn't a fluff bit; as a matter of fact, it had a cool, sorta raunchy chorus part. As I expected, there were protests.

I could then tell, at that time who was probably gonna split; and I'm glad it was the drummer, because I have an idea. I had a method to my madness, I'd find out who was gonna bolt, and...

Namaste

I then ask Elizabeth "did you write this recently, say after the other night?"

She shakes her head yes.

She has a sensual, breathy Sia voice; a younger Sia, like when she sang with *Zero 7* or the song *Breathe Me*; very trippy but sexy.

"Sometimes you write the best stuff from your inner core or soul. When you use your head you may have a technically nice song; but you have to create from somewhere deeper inside you; like your heart. You head gets in the way; so much noise and rules; it tries to make order and sense. Heart has more emotion and feeling; more spirit, you know what I mean? And try not to make something perfect. Perfect is the enemy of good enough."

"Nice arpeggio part; quiet at first then building into crescendo; I like it. I can't wait to work on it." I then explain how it is going to be a learning experience for her.

"You've got to communicate with the other instruments. You've got to tell them generally what you want; without stymieing their creative contributions. It's not like classical or traditional music where everything is scored; we are creating here."

"Don't you think that it's kinda stupid and simple," Elizabeth inquired.

"I think it's simple, yeah sure; but so? You're young, and inexperienced. You write what you know. I do like your title. You write what the heart feels to write; and what the heart wants the heart wants (I learned that from my music professor in college years ago). Besides, simple is just as valid as serious and complicated. I'm happy with this song; it's a start," I explain.

Oh no, I can see her starting to get that self-editing, overly self-criticizing attitude, which can shut a writer down.

"You've gotta pop your cherry with recording a demo song ya know?"

"This song is as good as any," I continue to explain to her.

I showed her how the chords she wrote, played a certain way could make the song more bluesy, à la Black Keys; or by changing the rhythm and strumming each string, more like a Cold Play song.

After a couple times going over the song, I saw she had a little trouble with singing some of the chorus section. I switched the B m chord to a D maj and she loved it; it worked well; it resolved so much smoother.

"Wow Woody, just changing out that one chord makes a massive difference," Elizabeth happily expressed.

I explained to her how all that music theory I studied in college has a pay-off; I knew that a D maj chord is a good sub for the B m chord.

The m8s said we're gonna become some No Secrets band; an obscure group of tweener girls who's claim to fame was a cover of Kim Wilde's song *Kids in America*. Kim Wilde was a Brit. Again, the fuck do they know; big babies.

That's why I was on the lookout for something new, those guys weren't contributing shit. I was doing all the writing and I was frustrated. I needed a new perspective; a female angle; hence, Elizabeth. Wait till they see I've got my eye on a female drummer; sheeeit, they are gonna wig out for sure.

I understand their attitudes though; it's the Yoko Ono syndrome. M8 falls for girl; girl convinces m8s she has musical talent; m8 insists girl be involved in band; m8 is deaf to her lack of talent; girl insinuates herself into the gig; band breaks up horribly. That is not the case here, I had to assure the m8s; we're not The Beatles.

The mutinous cacophony crested when I bought Elizabeth a 08 Shred – X carbon black Gibson Explorer for her birthday; the m8s know that that is one of my faves and why didn't I get it for myself. I had such a good fake out going on there for a while; I gave her a Hello Kitty phone case as her gift at first. After a couple minutes of what seemed to be sincere gratitude, I sprung the case on her; I feared she would faint – again. I told her that she can give it a dude name now and a custom finish; the m8s went ballistic at that. Well I hope she doesn't do it pink; so obvious.

Namaste

126

Chapter 9

Hens in da House:

Tina and I went to check out a girl drummer that Woody saw on a YouTube demo; she lives in Bay Ridge. Woody's not gonna drive into Brooklyn tonight in this snow storm; so it's gonna be like an econo lodge and mass transit for us.

"Cab, or subway Liz," Tina was asking me.

"Let's take the cab there" I choose.

"It's gonna take like an hour to get into Brooklyn by cab in this shit Liz."

"It's not that bad. It's not that far. It's okay, so let's do it," as I get in the cab, my face breaks through a wall of warmth. Tina slams the door behind her and tells the cabbie to go to 86th street in Bay Ridge.

"Is the girl still gonna gig in this weather Liz? What is her name?"

"Yeah sure, I called Alexandra before and she said it's still on."

"Man Liz, you ever think about being like a model. You're tall and really pretty, and man, you've got a killer bod and such pretty hair, wow, that hair! Maybe you could do that and the music."

"Thank you. Not interested in that; no time; don't care," I say hoping to get back to meditating on the sounds of the cab driving quietly, due to the snow, through the normally bone rattling streets of Manhattan; like white noise.

"Liz, you don't wanna find yourself all knocked up at such a young age," Tina's voice finally gashes through the soporific envelope of white noise and car heat wrapping over me. I am thinking whether I should tell her to call me either Elizabeth or E. I guess I'll let it go, for now.

"All it takes is for him to pop one off into you and voilà, you're on 16 and pregnant," she continues.

"Why would you say that shit to me Tina? Besides, I'm 15!"

"Even better, I mean worse; well, are you on the pill or something," Tina expresses with what I perceive as a preachy, motherly tone; which I find a bit condescending.

Again, another person who assumes I am naive, a hick, a ditz; I'm guessing it's the cross all pretty blonde girls have to bear.

"No. Why?"

"You could go to my doctor, if you need. She's really nice and would get you in real quick," Tina again with that tone.

"Why," I ask, but I think I know where this is going. She and Jerry came over to Woody's house and they caught us together in the bedroom.

"Woody and I didn't have sex. We haven't had sex. I haven't had sex. Since you must know my personal business Tina; but thank you for your concern," hoping my sarcastic tone would be the conversation ender.

"Alright Liz, but the way you two are, it's only a matter of time. It's better to be safe than sorry, right?" Tina expresses excitedly and then continues, "you want my OBG's name?"

"Yeah sure," I explain to Tina how I probably could use the name and number of an OBG since I didn't know one.

"You know, I think it takes like a week or so before they start working, so you shouldn't have sex until after that," Tina still with the tone.

"No problem. I'm not worried about that," I giggle so out of character for me.

"You say that now but you'd be surprised how these things happen Liz."

"I can't be surprised Tina, I do understand how these things happen. Want me to explain. I'm just screwing around." That came out bad. "I mean I'm just kidding around with ya," and now my brain is starting to hurt.

"My friends all call me either E or Elizabeth, and I consider you a friend Tina" I explain, proud of my tack.

"Woody always calls you Elizabeth, so it's Elizabeth sweetie," Tina now shifting to more of a social worker delivering a PSA voice. Shit, times like this I wish I brought my earbuds with me.

The heat and white noise begin enveloping me again. I'm staring out the cab window and see we are getting onto the Brooklyn Bridge before Tina speaks again:

Namaste

"A time will come, one of these days, the two of you will be goofing around, next thing you know, there will be hanky-panky," she says and I realize it's time to end this.

Tina's sex advice:

"You're still too young to have a kid."

"Actually, no I'm not. I'm 15, I think I'm fertile. I believe I'm physically fit and capable," I state matter of fact.

"You seriously want a child; now?"

"What. No. I was again, being obnoxious. I know what you mean. I want children maybe in like 4 or 5 years, when I'm 20 or 25; depends on what's going on."

"What about you? Are you gonna have kids Tina?"

"Yeah. Maybe like next year. We both wanna have three."

"Well, at any rate Elizabeth, you have a great sexual opportunity, if you ask me."

"Ima gonna regret this but what do you mean Tina?"

"Most of us, our first time is, well, sloppy, kinda clumsy; you know, high school boys aren't exactly Casanovas, though they think they are. My first time; sheeze, I was like 13; what a circus. Skip that, my first vaginal intercourse, I was 14; hmm, well that was clumsy also; you know how high school boys are."

"No, I really don't know; never had sex with a high school boy, or any boy. Anyway, both times with the same boy" I uncharacteristically find myself asking.

"Actually Liz, I'm sorry, Elizabeth, no; thank gawd. First there was pain as he, I think, tried the wrong hole. Then after he put it in the right place, like two seconds later it was done. Thank God I knew about this stuff, because he then freaked out with the blood and junk. It was funny and stuff, but you, my girl, have a grown man, with experience."

"Do you think that creeps guys out; you know, virginity and blood and junk,"

"Some guys are turned off, some guys are obsessed with it; it's weird."

Bay Ridge couldn't arrive quickly enough. I was shanghaied into Tina's personal sex advice column. All about how it's gonna feel, what to expect from him; what to expect from her; what not to expect; when to expect; how much, how little, how hard, how soft, how wet, how dry; me on bottom, me on top; back doors, styles, the bed, the floor, the tub; flipping over, sucking, humping, licking, squeezing; when not…, yada yada yada; kill me now. Ew! Ew! Ew! TMI, TMI!

I wanted to share with her about the night Woody and me almost had sex, but I couldn't break into her vocal blog. As she rambles on, I keep thinking of the intensity of the things I was feeling that night; how desperately I wanted him inside me. I'm starting to sweat, I think its sweat.

"Here ya are girls!" the cab driver mercifully interjects.

It's like 3am and after that night, I am totally wiped. I'm happy that Tina got us this descent hotel room to crash. I have never been in a club or bar before. Boys, men talking at us all night; thank God Tina was there. There were a couple hot guys that wanted to buy us drinks but Tina said we shouldn't; she said she didn't want to be contributing to the delinquency of a minor; and if a guy found out I was 15, who knows what would go on.

I think Tina finally fell asleep. I wanna call Woody now and tell him what I thought of Alexandra. .

That girl was a spectacular drummer, I think; but so did Tina. She's 16 and so fucking surprisingly hardcore, she could no problem pass for like 21. I can now see what Woody saw in her; and I realized that with her, we'll have like half a girl band.

"You okay Elizabeth?"

"Oh, thought you were asleep. Yeah, I'm fine, why?"

"I was laying here thinking of my first time in a club. I was 16 and with a couple friends. I remember drinking and throwing up all night."

"Did you take drinks from guys? Maybe they were roofied?"

"Yeah, lots of guys and lots of drinks. We had different guys buying us drinks all night. I drank way too much, that's why I got sick. So funny cause we definitely didn't look 18, not like you; and they still hit on us like crazy."

I explained to Tina about how I felt that night with Woody. When I told her how I was practically rolling my eyes back, how I shivered, then was burning up with sweat, how I got all wet, how I still think about it and want that again; she told me I experienced an orgasm.

Tina sits up in her bed and I sit there with her; she starts talking about boys and sex again.

Somewhere, the conversation veered into her sex experiences with girls.

HE texted, *SHE texted.*

All that sex talking with Tina, all night; now that's all I can think about
now. I gotta talk to him.

(HER phone)

Hey boy. Wanna know somtin

I resend it like 10 more times to have his alert sound wake him up.

(HIS phone)

(Bell Tower alert sound)

Im at your house, snowed in. whats up.

Is my mom and dad there?

Mom in b room dad idk. im in your br

Took video of alex want it now?

Namaste

N I'll driv in tmrow pic u up. Ok

Wanna ft?   U there? Whats up. I wanna FT

Woody can we facetime?

I just tried to ft u. storm

causing slow streaming I think.

I wanna c u naked.

I'm always pining 4 u!

I wanna c u naked & im naked now

Ur a goof. Stop teasing.

You naked xmit to me might b

Trouble, u no.

Sexting ok, no pics.

Shud have warned u bout Christina

U start ⋯   I luv u. U luv me?

#ILuvE

###ILU

U really mean that

You must Have been

told that by a zillion guys.

Hey mom, get off Woody's phone.

I guess it never meant anything to me till now, till you.

Wish you were here.

What r u wearing. O yeah u r naked

tina is asleep in the bed next to mine

What's Tina wearing?

Black sweats I think.

lick your hand and imagine it's

My warm, wet, tongue, where you

Wanna put it?

Namaste

Right there

I was making some noise and Tina woke up

Lets get her Involved.

christina, a piece of work!

Y?

Sex crazed school teacher re:

Looking for Mr Goodbar. Google it.

Your right bout Tina & Mr Goodbar. We took sum Xanny and she Is all sex talk.

Ooo u nasty gurls.

get back to sexting boy

Where do u want me to lick u now?

Hard cause little drunk

u r hard?

Hard = difficult

remember bath w candles,oil?

OiO yes, now hard

too bad 2nite w snow good time 4 that

U mean outside in the hot tub

yes!!!

I&i

What's that

I'll tell u l8r. How many chicks u had.

Sex with? Trap. Any answer trouble.

Come on, really.

Ill FT u now.

(Klaxon alert)

"Hi, wow that picture you sent me, you two looked so good. How was your journey in this weather hon?"

"I'm feeling really good right now. I can barely hear you, talk louder. So, how about the girls Woody? Tell us about that vast pool of sexual experiences."

"More like a kiddie pool. Shh, I don't wanna wake anybody up!"

"Ah, don't worry. I bet she's zonked out; right?" Elizabeth was asking about her mom. Should I come clean and admit that, yes, we were drinking and smoking together? No.

"You first; even just feel up's?"

"So boring, I got nothing. I wanna hear about your great romantic trysts; the threesomes; the dueling for a princess's honor."

"Oh, I can see by your geotag on that selfie that you're at the Best Western; is it a nice place, or is it a sleezebag, by the hour, hooker hotel?"

"Ew! It's fine. Stop deflecting!"

"Sorry Elizabeth, I got only awkwardness; I once made a girl bleed when having drunk sex. I accidentally bashed her in the nose with my head."

"One time this chick opened her drawer and asked which condom do I want? I didn't want to embarrass myself so I took the magnum sized; which then came off inside her. We spent half an hour searching around in there for it. Stories like that?"

"Ha, yeah that's so fucking funny."

"It takes a certain level of confidence to get two chicks hysterical laughing over a penis size story, especially when it's my penis they're hysterical about."

"This is a mine field; tell too many sex stories, I come off like a trollop."

"Speaking of size, you shoulda seen the freakin heels Elizabeth wore tonight," added Tina.

"Why, she hit the 6 foot mark?" I ask.

"Probably over that; but her fake ID said she was 5 foot 6, lucky she wasn't busted," Tina added.

At this time, Lilli came into the room; in front of the camera, "Hey there, I was wondering who you were talking to."

"Mom…"

Namaste

146

Chapter 10

Woody sends E on mission:

I asked Elizabeth to go talk to a drummer girl in Brooklyn. Christina asked to go along and Elizabeth was happy about that. We figured to avoid all that awkweirdness of an older guy recruiting a young chick nonsense; it's best that they go. Christina is quite the fangirl herself. At any rate, with this weather, it was decided for her to train into the city, meet up with Tina, and cab ride to Brooklyn. I'm sick of doing everything.

I was very impressed with the girl but, seeing her do a live gig will give a better impression. Although I do trust those two to judge if the girl okay, I'm uncertain of a female drummer; never mind that she's like 16. She had mad chops for a girl, but drums are a hardcore, marathon sport and I don't know many females who can handle a 2 hour set live. I've had drummers who lost 10 pounds in sweat in a night – it is totally barbaric.

One time my drummer popped some Adderall or ecstasy, and a 2 hour set was done in like an hour, so we had to jam and cover and repeat for the rest of the time. The drums are the heartbeat of the band; plus if you are playing along with a computer, they got to be able to play with a click in the ear – some guys can't do that.

So I'm hoping to have lightning strike again; then I'll just play keys, write and sing some. Yeah, I know it's so gimmicky; 2 hot young chicks in the band, but eye candy is <u>never</u> a bad thing; Hmmm, a band name, *iCandi*. Elizabeth will barf and say it sounds porno. My dreams of replacing my m8s with an all-girl harem are materializing, on schedule – ha! We shall see when I pick them up tomorrow in the city, depends upon the weather.

Crossing boundaries:

I struggle to recollect the previous night. Oh boy, I believe I'm in some trouble; there's a blondie sleeping next to me, and I'm not in *my* bed. She rolls towards my side. For a minute, in that hazy twilight when you are immersed in a dreamstate reality, and before you are conscious of real reality, I thought omigod, Elizabeth and I ….

My dream had manifested into the time when Elizabeth and I were in lying in bed, recuperating from writing and jamming for 12 hours straight; and some freaky bud.

A shock riffled through my brain when I noticed that I was in the buff; and the blondie, has now rolled on top of me, her breasts crushing against my chest.

The blurring clears from my eyeballs; Lilli is on top of me, draping her hair over my face; it weaves with my darker blonde strands.

Namaste

"What's the matter" she asks because she can obviously read my mind via my tensioning.

"Hah? Um. Everything is good." I had a hard time just to say her name, *Lilli.*

Fangirl, the Animal:

I haven't processed the situation yet; wasn't even sure who she was; I have almost cleared from my sleepy cloud; nearly blurted '*Elizabeth.*'

"It's okay, you don't have to apologize for wanting her instead," she said close to my ear and with a very wet whisper.

What? I thought, what mother says that about her jail-bait daughter? She must still be high.

I was flooded with the thought, *where is he? Her husb... her.. E's daddy?* I recall Elizabeth telling me about her dad's gun stash; oh fuck!

Sheeeit! A spectacular night of sex and passion with a chick I've fantasized about, has materialized, and now it is being fucked up by flooding my mind with thoughts of fear and loathing. I have certainly had a crush on Lilli from minute one.

I try and sit up.

She's having none of it.

Pinning me like a wrestler, she's now rearing back, pushing up with her hands on my chest and digging her nails into me, swinging her tawny mane vigorously, snapping her head to and fro. I thought, she's too wild, she's gonna snap me in half.

Her moans, her labored breathing betray her climax; her eyes roll back. Her grunting reveals her as the feral female creature ostensibly raised by wild beasts she becomes. The earth being 4 ½ billion years old, she is, at this moment deeply submerged in the greatest five seconds of that 4 ½ billion years; dynamically writhing and slithering in her primeval pool of boiling perspiration emanating from her bodily doorway.

She slumps forward, collapses onto me with a gasp, then a groan. Prostrate, splayed-out, and devoured. Expended and exhausted, the girl had sated her desires to excess. I was proud enough to roar, *I'm something, hah?* I'm thinking that you can't do better than that; speed of light man. We hit the speed of light and you can't go faster than that.

"Baby, you okay."

She shutters, "Wow, man, I am definitely okay, you?"

I smile and throw her off my chest. "Oh yeah, I am a-oh-fucking-kay baby doll!"

She flips over and drapes her arm back over my chest and I lie there staring up at…. Now I remember, this is her bedroom.

This had all began late last night, early AM. Smoked a doobie and drank some rum which led to lots of giggling and fooling around. Oh yeah, then Elizabeth called. Lilli seemed to get all very playful, which led to more rum and tickling and wrestling then foreplay and passionate fondling. I don't do well with bud – I don't know why I get so baked. Most times when I smoke, I get couch locked, but this time, I got all horny and energized. I think the playful girl also had something to do with us ending up dancing the horizontal tango.

My brain, unfortunately, had collected its scattered thoughts, and reality had completely metastasized into my fog – this is Elizabeth's mom! I just had a romp with Elizabeth's mom, in Elizabeth's house; in Elizabeth's fucking house. This has I don't know how many layers of fucked-up-ness to it. What a train wreck; I'm utterly flabbergasted.

Coo coo a choo,

Mrs. Robinson,

Jesus loves you more than you will know,

woe woe woe: mind's iPod.

The blizzard outside had not materialized quite as dramatically as the weather reports had claimed; yeah sure there is what looks like maybe half a foot or so, but not the two feet, white out, hurricane winds and ten foot drifts.

I blame the damn weather man for me ending up hooking up with basically my girlfriend's mother; sheeeit!

I could just tell Elizabeth: *girl, while waiting until you're legal, let me take a run at your mom, aight? Sure, no problemo.*

"Wow, ah man, howmi gonna deal with Lizabeth?" When Lilli said that I jerked, nay I jumped into a sitting position. Peeling off the rest of her body which had rusted on to mine, I kissed her softly on the head and bounced up to get dressed.

"I'm sorry Woody, didn't mean to freak you out like that. I'll make us coffee."

"Like what?"

"Freaking out about Lizabeth at this moment," she said to clarify.

"I mean, I shagged my daughter's fiancé."

"Why'd you say that Lilli?"

"You two practically cohabitate," she answers.

"You reminded me how I gotta pick her up. How is that freakin out?" I asked while getting confused over her freaking out over freaking me out.

"That's not what I meant; I know the relationship you two have."

"Coffee sounds great Lilli, thanks" I said as I placed my finger over her lips to bring a halt to that topic, too weird. I pondered that statement from Lilli; *relationship.*

What the hell did Elizabeth say to her mother? Was that jealousy I detected? Whoa, I'm in some freaky Lilli and Elizabeth sandwich and I'm literally lunchmeat. Which women is gonna kill me in my sleep most gruesomely. I really should just get fucking as far from here… Keep driving.

No Sleep Till, Brooklyn:

"You coming with" I asked Lilli who was still in the kitchen.

"You want me to?"

"Absolutely doll, I don't want to be alone; hold me!"

I had calmed down somewhat from the shock of appreciating my bewildering circumstances.

"Now I don't know if you're being a dick or not. Do you want me to come with you?"

"I swear on the bible, I want you to accompany me to Brooklyn. I really, really, really don't….. want to be by myself, driving all alone. Besides, I love your company anytime Lilli-san, you know that for real. It's gonna be a slow drive with the roads all fucked up like, I really do need you."

Oh man, she beams me that sexy smile with her emerald glazzies just like Elizabeth does; welcome to my fucking clownshow.

This is not what I brought her along to do, Lilli has been silent and stiff the whole drive. I am wondering who is Elizabeth gonna be most pissed at. Probably her mom; she already has hostility towards her. She'll see her mom as a harlot, horning in on us.

Familiar with Elizabeth's anger, I think we are all in danger.

Ménage à trois:

"You wanna discuss" Lilli finally cracks the silence.

"Actually, I want a benzo, of any variety, but I gotta drive."

"We're in Brooklyn, we're gonna be getting her soon" she whispers as if Elizabeth can now hear us.

"Look, I vote for don't ask don't tell, all right," Lilli shakes her head yes and says "it was just sex."

"I'm offended," I enquire after that word settles in, "just."

"Fight Club rules" I ask.

"What do you mean?"

"First rule in fight club…." I stop after she shakes her head.

"Am I a shitty mother?"

"What. No. You are a great mother; you have certain idiosyncrasies, but you are a wonderful mom. It's just that sometimes you are your own worst enemy; same as me."

After a few more blocks in stark silence we're at Elizabeth's hotel, then I say "Shitty wife."

"I'm not married," Lilli explains.

"Quibbles," I add; "and you know, I've got to tell Elizabeth, someday, soon."

"You're gonna blow the two of you up like that; and her father and I?"

"I hope not; but she'll hate me if I don't tell her and she finds out. She'll see it as allowing you to have something over on her – a secret. If I tell her, she'll be disappointed with me; she'll be angry with you – which is her default state anyway."

"There are times I wish there could be a *Men in Black* neuralyzer thingy..." I tell Lilli.

"Woody, have you two had sex?"

"You silly wabbit, if we had, I wouldn't tell – her mother!"

"Lilli, you've reared a wonderful young lady there. She's very mature emotionally. She's the only real adult amongst us fools. If this whole thing blows up, it will happen because that's what she decides is best for her. She has a strong self-preservation instinct. She makes good choices."

"I asked you about sex because she asked me no, she told me, she's moving in with you," Lilli pleaded.

"You fucked me to stop that!" I exploded. "She'll just move into the city, alone!"

"Lilli, you've got to stop running away from shit with those damn animals and hang with the people you love, baby doll. Get to know your daughter, and your fucking husband."

"You're right, she's gonna hate me, she's gonna tell Daniel," Lilli said all worried.

"I said she's gonna be angry with, not hate you – immense difference. She loves her mom; girlpower."

"It is really impressive just how ruthless she can be. She'd snap a shank off in anybody who got in the way of her dream, and step over their bodies," I said.

"150 years ago, people would travel anywhere on earth to strike it rich on a gold claim. Don't forget, getting around back then was daunting and extremely dangerous; both men and women; young and old. For a girl like Elizabeth, to go to New York or freaking Timbuktu, is no big deal. Shacking up with a nice guy like me in Queens is nothing if it moves her towards her goal; but she honestly likes me and I her, so it works out."

"You seem to really know her and care for her Woody, and I guess I appreciate that a lot. So then, you two like girlfriend boyfriend type of thing?"

"Well, I guess. But you're not officially gfbf until you proclaim it publically," I answer Lilli.

"I've seen her naked" I kinda just blurted out. After a good minute of quiet I continued, "Haven't gotten past 2nd base."

"Why did you see her nude?"

"I wanted her to prove that she had no ink on her."

"Why, does that matter?"

"We were talking. I thought that tats were passé, so establishment and conforming. She agreed, she stripped down... me to. We are both inkless."

I stretch out my arms and give Lilli a long, tight hug. We could feel each other through our thick coats; "that was a grand-slam at the ballpark hah Lilli."

We step onto the elevator to go up to Elizabeth's room to collect the girls.

I kiss her on the lips, and we continue to hug and kiss when the elevator jolts to the 3rd floor. Now I'm fretting over which girl is gonna wind up moving in with me; so many layers. I'm like some witless spider getting caught in a web of my own making.

Namaste

164

Chapter 11

Demo – lition:

The music demo is getting good responses and I think we have something happening really soon. We got a record company that is interested in a further recording. They're gonna set us up in London for a couple three months because they have some people there that they believe would work well with engineering and producing our stuff. I mean we could set up tons of gigs right now but I don't want to go that route if we don't have to.

I was thinking that we can somehow title the album in reference to my hot tub; since most of the material was composed whilst Elizabeth and I were chillaxing in the hot tub I have at my house.

Hot Tub Love Machine:

"Oh man, this is some good shit Elizabeth!" Alexandra takes a toke from a joint.

"Yeah my dad grows this at the farm in New Jersey. I think it's called Amnesia Haze or Purple Haze, ha something like that!"

"So how do you feel Alex?"

"Hmm, I think I feel comfortably numb E, ha."

After a grueling session of practicing and recording, writing and re-recording, remixing, re-composing, re-recording, it was now in the gloaming of the pre-dawn of a January morn. Alexandra and I have come outside, in Woody's backyard to get some fresh air, and to cool off. We both stood there, smoking the joint, without coats on, in the crispy 20 degree motionless air. There was the slightest sliver of a crescent moon. We could barely hear the guys in the studio replaying the music we just banged out; mostly we could feel the bass vibrate the ground.

"So E, who was that bleach blonde chick that I saw in the house?"

"Oh, that was Molly. She's like a cleaning lady."

"He has a nice place hear, how does he pay for it?"

"He used to work in Manhattan in some giant law firm as a computer security guy and he made a lot of money; enough to quit that so he could do music."

"He just started playing!" Alexandra asked.

"No, he's did it even when he worked. As a matter of fact, he writes music for media and TV stuff and made money with that. That's why he has the recording studio. He hooked me up with his agent and I sold a couple of weird songs I composed. I actually got my first pay in my account yesterday!"

"Speaking of agents, you're gonna need one to. Makes sense, Woody said since we're the teen girls of the band, if we become celebs, we might have to deal with like teen mags and acne cream and make-up commercials type stuff."

"You're right, never thought of that."

"You see yourself doing some Teen Vogue or Covergirl thing Alex?"

"Ha ha, fuckin yeah, ow!"

"Right. Some of that shit is fucked. They sign us up for some square shit, then we get on TMZ all smacked up with our vag hanging out like LiLo, ha!"

"You're killing me E! Or like some of the dudes getting caught on stage puking on the fans or falling off the stage!"

"Can't wait!"

After a while, the sweat which had moistened my clothing had begun to flash freeze; the dampness in my hair froze it taut. I look over at Alexandra and I could see the vapor emanating from her hair; I assumed she was starting to chill as I was.

"Ha ha, are you thinking what I am Alex?"

"The hot tub E?"

"Hurry up E, my fu fu fuckin ass is f f freezing off!" She said while we struggled, now naked, to fold the cover off, exposing the steaming Jacuzzi.

I take a final pull from the doobie, hand it to Alexandra, turn on the bubbling jets, and step into the warm boiling caldron.

"Ahhhhh…!" She exclaims as she follows me into the 102 degree relaxing heaven.

"Aw fuck E, we didn't bring our robes or towels."

"Whoops! Oh well Alex, we'll just have to strut out into the stark chill wet and naked."

Namaste

My senses are firing strange but cool info into my cortex; spiritual and profane.

The din of the hot tub bubbling, the delirium inducing heat, and the cannabis soon had me starring, trance-like into Alex's plate size brown eyes.

I had Alex figured out; fungirl, anything goes; typical 16 year old girl doing what is normally a boy's job: drummer girl, from a rough part of Brooklyn.

"We look like a couple alligators in the swamp with just our noses and eyes above the water line," Alexandra says, snapping the trance.

"You look so pretty Alex with your black hair all wet and framing your big brown eyes with the water line like that. You have really pretty eyes."

"Ah, that's so sweet E."

Her hand emerges from below the water reaches over and swipes the curtain of hair from my face. All the hues of her face become emphasized while wet; her olive skin, Hollywood white smile matching her eye white, the blackness of her pupils in their brown setting.

I reach over, grab her shoulders and our lips collide.

Beneath the surface of the bubbles, our hands are exploring each other. She traces her hand down my sternum and around each of my breasts, seemingly as if writing a message on me, punctuating on each nipple, which acts as on buttons; turning on deep sensations in the low parts of my body.

Being a noob, I would mimic on her what she would do on me. We moved to the bench part of the tub. She spread my legs with her hands and slid her leg in between and eventually sliding her thigh up and tight, grinding on me. I am lost for a while in a laser point right above her mouth and below her nose until I slam my eyes shut when she hits a certain spot, down there. I feel her hot moist breathe now in my ear.

I can feel my furious heart beating, flooding my body with pleasure hormones. After sampling the flavors of my face, she tastes my neck and is pressed against my breasts. I feel myself charged with goose bumps as she sucked on a sweet spot behind my ear, and under the water, things were going on. Then as I was grabbing her hair in culmination, the Jacuzzi timed out. Suddenly, the only sounds were our intake of breath, mixed with gasps; evident sounds of attaining both divine and wicked fulfillment.

The deep space like atmospheric temperature froze our breath into hovering ghosts, and glazed my wet body with ice when I stood up. I gasped sharply and submerged myself on a seat. The simmering of our bodies, and the lingering effect of purple or amnesia haze, dizzied my brain; or perhaps it was the sensual pleasures presented to me thanks to Alexandra. The heat was knocking me out.

"Elizabeth," Alex whispered softly.

I opened my eyes. I believe that I was having a micro dream.

"Alex, you are a true goddess of pleasure," I said in a delirium voice.

It was like a minute or two from the sun orb making its initial arrival.

"So E, are you ready to run into the house all wet and naked?"

"I'll get my phone out of my pocket and call Woody to bring us robes or towels; it's really fucking painfully cold when you stand up."

"Alex, are you gay?"

"Hm, I don't think so, are you E?"

"Maybe we're like bipolar or something Alex."

"Bipolar? How do you come to that?"

"Jeez, I mean bisexual."

"E, maybe we're bipolar bisexuals!" Alexandra says jokingly.

"I liked what we did and all Alex. I thought about when Woody and I are…"

"Well Woody always says all sexual feelings are in the brain anyway. Most people are wired to desire the opposite sex, otherwise we wouldn't exist; homos are wired in a different way and since there are like 9 billion of us, we can tolerate homos; we not gonna go extinct from that."

"You know Alex, wow we really do have one good looking, sexy, rockin band, dontcha think?"

"Yep."

Student teacher.

"Thanks for bringing us these robes Tina."

"Sure, no problem Elizabeth. I didn't want you two to have to walk in naked in front of the guys."

"Yeah, thanks Tina."

"You're welcome Alex."

"Fuck the nakedness, we didn't want to freeze our asses off, it's cold!" Alex told Christina.

"I've moved in here with Woody," I told Tina and Alex.

"What. How'd that happen?" Tina asked.

"I asked him if I could, and he said yes, end of story."

"Come on dude, there's got to be more to it than your usual robotic Elizabeth talk," Tina said.

"How's that work at your age, with a guy his age," Tina asked.

"What about your parents, are you gonna tell them or what, elope or something," Alex asked.

"I've stayed at his place plenty of times."

"Wait. Like you've slept with Woody," Alex asked.

"Once, but now I stay in the other bedroom."

"What, you're talking about that time Jerry and I walked in on you two…?"

"Yes Tina."

"Well get this, in an effort to kinda break us up, my mom slept with Woody."

"Get the fuck outta here! No way," they both exclaimed.

"You mean she outright fucked him," Alex scoffed.

"That's how fucking crazy of an environment I live in. Most girls have to worry about other girls, maybe even their own girlfriends stealing their guy. Not me. I gotta worry about my own mother!"

"What did you say to Woody; I mean, he cheated on you," Christina growled.

"He's the one who told me about it; before we were paramours; it was the time you and me went to Brooklyn to see you Alex."

"Is your mom like really hot," Alex queried.

"Wow; this is like too weird Elizabeth, way too weird. I'm worried about you. You're too young to get involved in all this," Tina's concern is becoming obnoxious; like the teacher she is.

"That's why I'm living with Woody. Man, you have no idea… I wanna get away from that crazy shit and have my own life. You should be worried if I stayed there!"

"Wow, you know what would really be weird E, is if Woody knocked both you and your mom up, woa man that'd freak me out. I mean he'd be the baby daddy to your half-sister and your baby, holy shit, ha!"

"Ew, fucking Alex you suck, you know!"

"My fucking mother is sterilized; something like that!"

"You can immerse yourself into your music I guess! Well, what did your mom say," Tina inquired.

"She helped me pack my truck up. She's fine with it all. It's all good now teach."

"Wow Elizabeth, I'm totally wigging out for you two. I mean your mom should have been like hands off Woody," Alex says while hugging me.

"I teach girls not much younger than you and I can't imagine them being close to leaving home, shacking up, hanging with music guys!"

"Sex, drugs, rock n' roll, right E," Alex bellows.

"I know you're worried that I might be one of those teen girls; fucked up by my parents; with low self-esteem; grabbing onto the first guy that shows me affection; especially an older man – a *father figure*. You're afraid I'm being manipulated because I'm young and naive. You're concerned that I'm gonna get knocked up; you're troubled I'm a drug addict. I've heard all this from my mom, from my friends; next I'll hear it on CNN."

"Those are legitimate concerns Elizabeth."

"Life if full of concerns Tina; my main concern is I don't want to be alone; I want to be happy. Woody and I are happy together; besides, we sleep in separate rooms – I know you've been thinking about that since you caught us that night. That was a one-time deal – believe me."

Bottle of Red, Bottle of White:

Elizabeth and I have asked her mom and dad out to dinner to describe to them of both the recording deal and the London stuff. I have already told Lilli that I told Elizabeth about that thing of ours. I knew that Elizabeth would forgive me because she would believe that her mom ensnared me. I hope that being away in London will give time to heal the mother daughter schism.

I'm wearing a nice charcoal suit, a cool dark blue fitted dress shirt with a sweet beige and red paisley silk tie; and black dress shoes. Lilli has only seen me as a punk rocker or farmer.

Why do we have to spring it on them? Surprise! Because this is the way Elizabeth wants to do it. I told her to follow up immediately the statement we're engaged with *and I'm not pregnant!*

"I finally get a chance to actually have a conversation with your father. I know you've told me about his job in the computer field, I can talk to him about the years I spent working at a big multi-national law firm in Manhattan working computer security."

"Try not talking to him that much. He doesn't care, he won't be impressed," Elizabeth stated with a pathos sending shivers through me.

"You are so bleak about him; or is that pure, guttural hate?"

"I just know him."

"I used to have top level clearances due to some of the client files I had access to; like major corporate people, entertainment industry, government people. He'd be impressed with all that stuff; I used to travel to Europe and South America."

"He's not that big a deal; he works for small businesses and he's a technician, not a manager like you were Woody."

"I'm telling him my resume to impress him with my skills; you know, dads wanna know that their future son in law would be a good provider and stuff. He doesn't know anything about me, remember. I always found that, well, problematic."

"I'm fucking telling you you're wasting your time so don't fucking bother, just drop it."

"Okay. Did you call your mom?"

"Yes Woody, I sent her a text and explained."

"Well how much did you tell her."

She showed me her phone screen:

hey mom. Be by round 6pm.

Where we goin?

Resturant in town, Luv U, soon, bye.

Luv U

"Are you gonna tell her as soon as we get there, or what?"

"I'll wait. But she's gonna see the ring. So I guess I could tell her that."

"Elizabeth, that's gonna stop her heart. You can't just nonchalantly spring '*Hi mom. I'm fifteen and I'm engaged to this guy 11 years older than me'.*" I tell Elizabeth while still astonished at her blunt tactics.

"Elizabeth, you are exhibiting some mental illness behaviors – should we reevaluate what we are about to do?"

"I'm fine. I'm a little tense too; but I wanna do this, now."

Namaste

"Um, did you take anything babe?"

"No. I wanted to, but decided no."

"What about telling her we got to go to London for a couple months to do the album." I explain.

"You know, give the good news first before lowering the boom." I have to plead to use thoughtfulness so everybody feels good.

"Speaking of news, you need to choose what you're gonna do about your separate deals."

"What deals?"

"You know; remember I was talking to you about the chick from like Teen Vogue or something who wants to contact you. You need to hire someone, like an agent, to deal with things that are just you. Teen Vogue, Seventeen, you know like teen mags and tweener rags. You are, after all, a teen; and you are glamorous and interesting, and most importantly, you are up and coming!"

As we drive, Elizabeth picks some Pearl Jam station on the Sirius that I re-upted.

"There's a cool station that plays 70's rock. 90's or 70's are golden decades for guitar rock. The 80's were fucked." I tell Elizabeth.

"There was some stuff in the 80's" Elizabeth pleads her case.

Elizabeth parks on a station playing:

'Pour some sugar on Meee,' I sing.

'Pour some sugar on me, We are both singing.

'c'mon fire me up,' me.

'Pour your sugar on me,' both of us louder and smiling big.

'I can't get enough'

'I'm hot,

sticky sweet,

from my head to my feet, yeah,' I sing this and we burst out; that was relaxing.

"Alright, there were some cool songs in the 80's," I concede to Elizabeth.

Chapter 12

Life is but a Dream:

When we get to the restaurant, Lilli is waiting at the front. Elizabeth is gonna tell her that we plan on doing this after she turns 16. I told her not to since, honestly, we don't know all the logistics and legalities of this; I hope this works out.

"Where's your father," I ask Elizabeth.

"He called and said he's running late and he'll meet up with us." Lilli explained.

"Can't keep your gloves on all night" I say to Elizabeth as we are seated.

"I'm gonna get that butter coffee they have after we eat," I tell Lilli as we look over the menus.

"Mom," Elizabeth says while removing her glove and showing the ring to Lilli.

Namaste

"We have good news about our music," Elizabeth says while Lilli is still reacting to the engagement reveal.

We are here and the wait staff is placing our drinks in front of us; and I have an interesting notion of how we are a literal énage a trois; wow, I pleasured both these girls.

Elizabeth is dishing out the double whammy of news to her mom; so impassive.

"Hey Elizabeth, here's Daniel," I say looking at him rushing in.

"Ow, that fucking hurt!" I shout as I seem to hear another loud crash.

I think I hear Lilli yelling at Daniel something about …

"Nigga Pa-leeze, no you didn't just shot me!"

Newspaper report.

Newspaper report:

Sommerville restaurant opens day after shooting death

Customers, staff return after man is killed in front of patrons; another shot and critical.

By Laura White

The Sommerville restaurant where 2 men were shot Saturday during dinner hours reopened Sunday to a busy brunch crowd as shaken wait staff tried to push the horror of the prior night's events behind them.

Namaste

Daniel Erickson, 46, of 10 Lincoln Street Sommerville, New Jersey had entered the restaurant at approximately 7:00 pm last night where his live in partner, his daughter, and family friend Woody Weber, 26, of Queens, New York were dining.

According to Sommerville Police Cmdr Bruce Benson, Erickson approached the booth where Weber was sitting and shot him, several times, at point blank range. He then turned the gun on himself and fired one shot under his chin. Erickson was pronounced dead at the scene. Weber is at Sommerville General Hospital in critical condition and in a coma.

Beef:

I am thinking about the first time I saw Lilli. I thought wow, what a smoking hot babe, I wished, nay I prayed that I could bang her for sure. Oscar Wilde said: *When the Gods want to punish us, they answer our prayers.*

I don't know if I am in a coma or dead right now; I've never been either before. I often wondered though, do the dead know they are dead. I am aware that I am not alive; at least alive as I have always known it.

He came at me, all gangster; like in the Godfather when Michael Corleone comes out of the bathroom high on vengeance; gat held sideways. At least I didn't have linguine dripping out my mouth. He had legit beef; banging both his girls. That was crazy but not blasting crazy. I had some good stuff going. All I hope is baby girl moves on; and she will.

Namaste

My thoughts seem to be my thoughts, but infused with occasional random concepts. Sort of like the commercials interrupting a TV show; only not advertisements at all. I just got flashed with the silly thought of the phenomena of Manhattanhenge; where the sun lines up with the east-west Manhattan grid. Silly indeed.

I seem to remember a pain striking me before I ended up here; and I remember Daniel rushing towards me. If I am dead, I think he had something to do with it. I can think of a couple of reasons he would have beef with me. His daughter is shacking up with me; and oh yeah, that incident with his baby momma. If this is so, he should be mindful of Confucius; *before you embark on a journey seeking revenge, dig two graves…*

If I am dead, then I surely am in hell because I am without Elizabeth. Any time spent without her, is hell, whatever state.

I had told Elizabeth all about that night with her mother and all, around the time I realized that I seriously cared for her; as a girlfriend. Elizabeth and I hadn't really bonded yet when all that went down; and I did kinda him have a crush on Lilli. I honestly didn't know exactly what kind of relationship Lilli and Daniel had going on. I never heard of nor saw any affection, or at least any warm feelings between those two. I don't think she cooed into his ear the way she would with me; it would send shivers down my spine.

Elizabeth appeared to just brush it off. She believed that her mother seduced me; in fact, that Lilli was the aggressive one that night.

Elizabeth and I have spent nearly every waking hour together for the past 8 months; and some dreaming hours. That's gotta be like 2 years' worth of regular couple's courtship time.

Namaste

I know that she is in love with me; I know I'm in love with her; we've declared this to each other – many times.

I think we both liked the whole outlaw-ness of getting hitched; so Bonnie and Clyde; or at least Sonny and Cher.

That was a grabbin the fire moment again; although, not exactly very romantic. I had no idea what I was doing; I've never even come close to a marriage proposal before.

"Should we take a selfie with you showing the ring and post it, or should we have a more formal sit down with the in-laws?" I ask. We eventually decided on the latter.

Wait…

Glossary:

If you come across a word, phrase, or reference that(which) you do not know, highlight it and Google it; do the work. Or, if you get stuck on a word or perhaps an obscure phrase, PM me on my facebook **https://www.facebook.com/jaamzshow?ref=aym t_homepage_panel**

Namaste

ELIZABETH PLAYLIST ON SPOTIFY, HERE'S THE GUTS OF THE LIST.

ETERNAL FLAME	THE BANGLES
ROLLING IN THE DEEP	ADELE
HEAD OVER FEET	ALANIS MORRISETTE
DREAMS	THE CRANBERRIES
LINGER	THE CRANBERRIES
CLOSE TO ME	THE CURE
LOVE SONG	THE CURE
TIME WON'T LET ME GO	THE BRAVERY
BOHEMIAN LIKE YOU	DANDY WARHOLS
THE LAST HIGH	DANDY WARHOLS
I REMEMBER	DEADMAU5
NO CARS GO	ARCADE FIRE
THANK YOU	DIDO
COOL KIDS	ECHOSMITH
LIGHTS	ELLIE GOULDING
MISSING	EVERYTHING BUT THE GIRL
HAYLING	FC KAHUNA
SWEET ESCAPE	GWEN STEFANIE
EDGE OF THE OCEAN	IVY
SWAMPED	LACUNA COIL
THE FEAR	LILLYALLEN
LOVE COME DOWN	EVELYN CHAMPAGNE KING
HABITS	TOVE LO
PASSING BY	ZERO 7
SYNAESTHESIA(FLY AWAY)	THE THRILLSEEKERS

Namaste

6 UNDERGROUND	SNEAKER PIMPS
GLORY BOX	PORTISHEAD
WHEN I'M SMALL	PHANTOGRAM
GOLD GUNS GIRLS	METRIC
TEARDROP	MASSIVE ATTACK
MINT	KATHLEEN EDWARDS
THE BACHELOR AND THE BRIDE	THE DECEMBERISTS
UNBREAK MY HEART	TONI BRAXTON
AT SEVENTEEN	JANIS IAN
DO I WANNA KNOW	ARCTIC MONKEYS
SOME NIGHTS	FUN.
HEART WANTS WHAT IT WANTS	SELENA GOMEZ
SEASON OF THE WITCH	DONOVAN
GRAPEVINE FIRES	DEATH CAB FOR CUTIE
WICKED GAME	CHRIS ISAAK
THE REASON	HOOBASTANK
TURN ME ON	DAVID GUETTA(FEAT. NICKI MINAJ)
HEROES (WE COULD BE)	ALESSO FT. TOVE LO
SAN FRANSISCO	JILL SOBULE
IN THE WAITING LINE	ZERO 7
UNDER THE BRIDGE	RED HOT CHILLI PEPPERS
ONE HEADLIGHT	THE WALLFLOWERS
CLOSING TIME	SEMISONIC
MOTHER MOTHER	TRACY BONHAM
TODAY	SMASHING PUMPKINS
FELL ON BLACK DAYS	SOUNDGARDEN
BIG YELLOW TAXI	JONI MITCHELL
COME AS YOU ARE	NIRVANA
EVERLONG	FOO FIGHTERS
PLUSH	STONE TEMPLE PILOTS
YOU OUGHTA KNOW	ALANIS MORISSETTE
FADE INTO YOU	MAZZY STAR
CREEP	RADIOHEAD
KARMA POLICE	RADIOHEAD
DECEMBER	COLLECTIVE SOUL
THE WORLD I KNOW	COLLECTIVE SOUL

Namaste

ALIVE	PEARL JAM
BLACK	PEARL JAM
DOLL PARTS	HOLE
BREATHE ME	SIA
WHERE IS MY MIND	PIXIES
IN THE WAITING LINE	ZERO 7
ECLIPSE	PINK FLOYD
FIRST TIME EVER I SAW	ROBERTA FLACK
LOVE TO LOVE YA	DONNA SUMMERS
IT'S TOO LATE	CAROLE KING
BIG YELLOW TAXI	JONI MITCHELL
COMEDOWN	BUSH
DON'T SPEAK	NO DOUBT
PLUSH	STONE TEMPLE PILOTS
ATOMIC	BLONDIE

Elizabeth *Click to hear playlist on Spotify. It's like, um, 5 hours plus long; Should take 5 hours or so to read this novel. E and I really dig this list!*

Namaste

www.ingramcontent.com/pod-product-compliance
Lightning Source LLC
Chambersburg PA
CBHW071714140626
46557CB00011B/133